Leslie Wilson was born in Nottingham in 1952 of a German mother and a British father. Brought up bilingually, she studied German at Durham University in order to get closer to her German cultural heritage. She has lived in England, Germany and Hong Kong and now lives in Reading. She has worked in further education, as a translator, as an unpaid journalist for a local community newspaper, as a mother and in the anti-nuclear movement. Her work has been published in the *Guardian, Orbis*, and *Women Live*. Leslie Wilson is currently working on a novel centred around a seventeenth century witch trial. She has two daughters.

LESLIE WILSON

Mourning is
Not Permitted

The Women's Press

First published by The Women's Press Limited 1990
A member of the Namara Group
34 Great Sutton Street, London EC1V 0DX

British Library Cataloguing in Publication Data
Wilson, Leslie
  Mourning is not permitted.
  I. Title
  823.914 [F]

  ISBN 0-7043-4256-1

Typeset by AKM Associates (UK) Ltd, Southall, London
in Baskerville 10½/12½
Printed and bound by BPCC Hazell Books Ltd,
Member of BPCC Ltd, Aylesbury, Bucks,
England.

For my daughters,
Kathy and Joanna

This desire to know is perhaps finally a way of loving.
Susan Griffin

1

'Look, said Anna, 'there is a repeating pattern, only it modifies as it goes through.'

There was that day I ripped twenty pages out of my history textbook while the teacher was dictating notes on the Weimar Republic. The other girls giggled and gasped – I'd done it quite openly, with my eyes on the teacher, and I could see hers, staring at me from behind her thick glasses. I knew she wouldn't be able to deal with me. She could deal with chattering, or laziness, but not with me. She asked me why I'd done it, but I wouldn't say because the other girls were listening, so she sent me to the headmistress. I was fourteen.

There I was again, the difficult girl whose rages and argumentativeness had to be explained by the broken home she came from, the girl whose mother's paintings were good enough for one to be hung as a print in the school art room. Which argumentativeness, along with my brilliance, already had me lined up for the open scholarship to Somerville. She put her determinedly patient hands on the table in front of her and asked why in her turn, 'Why, Karin, did you do such a thing?'

Out it came, how I'd been reading what the book had to say about the Blitz, that the Germans were war criminals because they had bombed British cities. Where, I demanded, did that leave the British, when my mother had dug burned-up babies out of the rubble of Berlin? When she herself had been trapped in the wine cellar of a blazing hotel, where they stole the champagne when it got too hot and found themselves roaring drunk and vomiting so that now she couldn't even see a bottle of the stuff without shuddering? When my grandmother had dug out her best friend and seen her stomach in tatters. And the book claimed the British had fought the war for the Jews. But this woman –

Miss Radford said that wanton destruction didn't solve anything. I asked her to tell that to Bomber Harris. She sighed. She said I was too sensitive and should take the chip off my shoulder – she didn't suggest how. I knew I'd put ants in her pants – I always did, was always antagonistic, though I really liked her. But she didn't have that dreadful barbed fence between herself and her heritage: it was all there, uncomplicated, behind her, around her. To give her credit, she always let me talk, maybe hoping to discover what it was really all about, because I kept turning up in her office, and each time she had to find something to say. She didn't believe in punishments, and she was far too much in awe of Anna to write to her about my behaviour, or mention it when Anna honoured them by showing up at parents' evenings. It remained between myself and the teachers. This time Miss Radford refrained, very pointedly, from making any comment on the issue of the Jews. She was right. Nothing had been solved.

I could have dealt with it the way Peter did – that might have been easier. If my brother says it's nothing to do with him, why can't I do the same? Why can't I believe him when he says it was nothing to do with his breakdown? Well, what is it to me now, when everyone in my family who lived through it is dead? It does me no good, though – and I can't really believe it did Peter any good – to deny the savage reality of what happened before I was born, that dark thread that wove itself into me through Anna and through Helene, my grandmother, my Omi. And my mother was a great painter and a diabolically difficult woman, and my grandmother was a depressive whom my mother insisted on taking out of mental hospital against everyone's advice, who cared for Peter and myself so Anna could paint. I loved them both, so I attacked the history book. That's simple, at least.

I always knew Anna was beautiful, but I had to wait till Helene was dead before I realised quite how beautiful my grandmother had been, even as I knew her, when her eyes had been somehow bleached by shock treatment and her pupils pinned small, never to dilate again. There was always in her expression a slight, fearful shrinking – she had beer so terribly hurt – at the same time her face was full of integrity. With her grey hair pinned back into a knot at the nape of her neck, she looked very like photographs of Virginia Woolf, and I wonder if mental illness imposes a landscape on the face that transcends individuality?

Not strong enough to face what came to her? Plenty of people endured worse, and survived, and it was my grandfather who had been beaten and imprisoned by the Gestapo. She got him out, though. She told me about those months when she went tapping up and down streets and stairs in her black silk dress and uncomfortable shoes, her eyes veiled with the hovering dots under the little hat, going from one important person to another. I have other pictures in my mind, Helene lying to the Gestapo when they arrested her and Erich after the Stauffenberg plot, Helene staggering away from the apartment the Russians had thrown her out of, her wounded nephew Josef on her back, Helene, who later became a vegetarian, carving chunks of meat out of a dead horse while the battle raged in Berlin.

In my dreams she's incredibly old, frail, feather-light, and she's living somewhere in my house and has been there for years. I've never noticed her, or the things she's been doing for me around the house. I've never even thanked her for baby-sitting. Now I go to find her. There she is at her sewing machine, the treadle neither Anna nor I could manage, but Helene keeps it going, her thin hands, with their swollen knuckles and high veins, shaking slightly as they guide the material through. She's making something for me, I don't know what.

It hurts. This is the crazy thing. It hurts. I wake up and lie in the darkness wishing I could cry, and I can't – it's as it was when I went to identify Anna, and I stood there quite calmly saying yes, I recognise this, and yes, that was hers, only I couldn't take in anything they were telling me about what would happen with her body, and Meg had to remember for me. The pain knots in my stomach and chest, like fear, and I shiver. And yet it's seventeen years since her death. (Eight months since Anna was killed.)

The curly-haired toddler I once was went with Anna to the pretty black-and-white Rhineland town we were never allowed to name, because for Helene the name meant hell. To the institution her husband had thrown her away into while he made a new life for himself with gold-toothed, wealthy Sybille. I can't remember Helene's tears, her voice begging Anna to take her away. Is it possible that it made no impression on me? I always disliked my grandfather.

Why is it coming up round me like floodwater? Now, when so many years have passed?

There is a repeating pattern in the two pictures she painted for this room. It is pattern, along with light and colour, that makes her work unforgettable. I didn't notice that progression when she brought them out of the car and unwrapped them among the packing cases, dashing Donald's hopes of cosiness and a flowered suite, since everything else in the room would have to be right for those pictures. She painted them for me, especially for me, and while I trembled with pleasure Donald scowled because he had been excluded, then brightened when it occurred to him we'd need a burglar alarm. Oh, he loves them when we entertain his colleagues and business contacts. Now I have this room, coloured in neutral shades to enhance them and a few beautiful objects. 'Living in an art gallery,' said Donald. Anna liked it. Leaving a tiny terrace for a huge Victorian semi we could barely afford had its advantages when I could escape clutter, especially the sort of antiques Donald is drawn to.

'You're your mother's daughter,' he said irritably. He was right, and there is no escape. There is a pattern, irregular, with variations, but the basic motifs come again and again. You watch them as your own children grow, and you see your past re-enacted, and sometimes it gives you pleasure, and sometimes pain, and sometimes it almost destroys you. I'm afraid of destruction. When I see my own face in the mirror, and see Helene's eyes, her nose, her pattern of lines on my brow, the goose walks over my grave. But destroy myself or not, I have to understand.

The phone. Damn. I'm certain it's someone I don't want to speak to. So why don't I just let it ring?

Peter. I was right. He's phoning from his bookshop. Polite enquiries about our health, how is Sally settling down at school, did we have a good Easter in Greece (disapproving note, and now he gets down to it). I'm neglecting our father. Dad has been complaining, saying I don't care about him.

I snap at Peter that if Dad and Edna had more tolerance for the children they'd see me more often, that he has Ruth always on hand to look after Julian, Emma, and Henry, whereas Donald is out of the country so much – Peter concedes this point (though it gripes him) and, he agrees, it's different for Donald.

Now I'm furious with both of them, Donald and Peter and their nauseous, sanctimonious solidarity. I'd like to knock their heads together, but that's only a side issue: do I want to visit my father and Edna?

And Peter said that if Dad dies tomorrow I'll regret it for the rest of my life. (Dead, and never called me Mother?)

The sunshine is laid out at my feet in coloured squares and rectangles, making almost exactly the same pattern as used to shine through the upstairs back window when we lived in Kendal. It was spooky and pleasurable to find it in the front door of this house. I'd like to see the fells again and the grey, dour buildings, and part of me even wants to see Dad. Besides, I'd be able to do a lot of thinking on the train: the rolling wheels are a mind-releasing drug for me.

Peter says, 'Karin, sometimes it looks as if you don't want to admit he's your father.'

Don't botch it, Peter. I might change my mind about going this weekend.

Donald wants to know why I'm ringing up in the expensive time. I tell him it's up to me how I spend my money, and he says I seem to think it's there to burn, so I tell him he's the one who's wasting time on the phone. I tell him I think I ought to go and see Dad, that this weekend is clear, and that I don't want to take the children.

As I await his reply, what began as an ultimatum becomes a request for permission. When *he* doesn't have to ask *my* permission to go away. 'Oh, darling, would you mind looking after the children on your own while I nip over to America for three weeks?'

He thinks his occasions are necessary, mine are not. They don't stand up to his form of cost-benefit analysis, where benefits have to be financial, or potentially so. All the same, I can sense the wriggling, threadwormy uneasiness in his bum because he's not the only moneybags any longer – the unstated control of my dependency has been wiped out. He might have guessed Anna would do this to him.

He makes a small counter-attack: he says we ought to talk about what I'm going to do with my time, now Sally is at school. I refuse to answer. He can't pursue it when his own time is ticking away on the meter, unjustified minutes. End of phone call, and a lingering sense of his displeasure.

This is my husband. Thirty-nine years old, attractive; director of the successful microbiology company he helped found in Oxford; charming to outsiders, especially women; most times, even now, good in bed. But I don't like him any more.

I am moving onto forbidden ground, this patch of carpet on Blackwell's floor, in front of these books that Anna said were all lies.

'They talk as if we, every one of us, was responsible. We never even knew. An open prison, that's what they said. For re-education. It's a German who wrote it? What difference does that make? They go over and over it, and what good does it do? Haven't we suffered enough?'

If I became convinced they had good reason to know, what will that do to me?

Helene said, 'They used to whisper about something called KZ.' I can hear her fearful voice even now, the whisper coming out as it must have done then when they began to talk about the camps; she even looked over her shoulder. But maybe she didn't connect it with the Jews, only with her husband's beaten body and knocked-out teeth. And her tailor, who made a joke about Hitler's celibacy (Helene, of course, didn't tell me the details, but I can guess) and came back from three months' protective custody with no finger-nails, unable to walk straight or stop weeping till he died a few weeks later.

Or do their words translate that it was better not to know? Fear puts up barriers that are more effective than barbed wire.

And again, the thought seems an attack on them, and I fall back, appalled at myself, Anna's voice in my ears: 'You? What difference does it make to you that she's dead? You've got your own life to lead now. Go on, you'll feel better when you're back at Somerville.'

Whoever else I shocked, Omi must never be shocked, must be protected because she was so vulnerable. Am I to abuse her, joining her husband and the psychiatrists who said she was violent? I, who hate myself for every childish outburst of anger against her? She wasn't violent. She was too gentle for her own good.

Shall I look at the books on the shelves?

My daughters are both dark. Would she have been unhappy about that? She was so pleased that I was blonde; oh yes, it meant something to her. I brought a black kitten home once, and she was so upset even *I* didn't want to keep it. They have Donald's colouring, and Elisabeth's hair is straight like

Donald's, but Sally, with her black eyes and her curls, looks like Bernt.

Bernt, who looks like his mother, who looks like her father, who looked so Jewish that he was beaten up in a dark alley one night in 1937 and joined the SS for self-preservation. And Bernt made his loathing for his grandfather so obvious the old man told Tante Maria never to bring the insolent young dog to visit him again.

Sally is delicious, I can't resist her, the smell, the feel of her, her cheeky little face, her hands patting and sometimes thumping me, the way she can make me laugh when I'm angry. Surely Helene wouldn't have rejected her because of her looks? But then when Bernt and his mother and father came to visit us at my great-aunt's in Bad Godesberg, why did Helene go to sit in her room? What was contained in her fear of them?

'And the Jews were taken away from their homeland because they killed Jesus, and were condemned to wander the world and never have a homeland again.' It was years before I realised that Jesus, too, was a Jew. And so? Plenty of people in this country don't like Africans and Asians. Does that mean they'd send them to the gas chambers if they had the opportunity? Ah, but what would they do if someone else took them away?

Helene sheltered three Jews – her neighbours – on Kristallnacht. She was afraid of Josef because he'd become a doctor. And she couldn't have seen Maria and Bernt on their own.

Anna told me, 'We never knew. When we found out at the end of the war, Omi wouldn't believe it. We thought they were all being deported to Poland.'

God, if only I was all British. Then I too could tut at what other people have done, and be sure it would never happen here. My schoolmates weren't tormented by these political complications.

I can hear Anna's voice again: 'Haven't we suffered enough?'

She would go to her studio, and I wouldn't see her for several hours, maybe not till the next day. I knew better than to disturb her.

2

My father is tall and lean, he has iron-grey hair and a long face that I now recognise as handsome. His skin is loose on his face and his clothes hang loosely on his body, but Edna keeps both in good condition. He sits, talking to me, while Edna bustles, interrupting our ritual exchanges about the journey.

'Let me bring you a cup of tea, Karen,' (firmly pronounced the English way). 'Oh no, you don't like tea, do you?' (her voice making it clear that this is a sin). 'Coffee? It's only instant, I'm afraid, dear,' (this last conveying, as always, no affection). 'I'll get you a cup of tea, Alan.' Edna, who was my father's secretary, bought shares in his prestige right from the start, sinking everything of her own in the investment, and she's made herself content with the small return they yield her.

As for me, I must be tolerated and placated for his sake, though I've always been troublesome, often obnoxious, keeping my room in a mess when I stayed there, sitting playing the guitar, lost to the world, when I'd been asked to set the table or help with the washing-up – and there, right in front of me, under my feet, is the rug they had to buy after I emptied the bottleful of permanent red ink over the carpet. I was thirteen. I can see her crouched there, weeping, scrubbing away at it, demanding that I be sent back to my mother, myself half-hoping, half-dreading that Dad would do it, and when he refused I screamed for half an hour. No-one could stop me until I had vented all my rage and bewilderment, and they stood round disliking me, Peter, my father, and Edna, quite helpless, every one of them, in spite of their threats. I had just got my first period and Edna had complained about the blood on the sheets – not unkindly, but she never had to do very much to set me off.

My father suggests we go for a walk once we have drunk our tea/coffee. The same idea, as always, to get us out, away, to free Edna from me.

My dislike is, it seems, as indelible as the ink, though edged with a fuzzy shadow of guilt because she's a woman. She's a collaborator: she licks her chains and claims to like the taste. Through her, and with her connivance, my father can despise those parts of himself he hasn't been able to destroy, like the crochet-skirted doll who broods so primly on top of the spare toilet roll.

She says if we want our walk we'd better get out before it rains. My father rises obediently (you give them the occasional illusion of power, and the system works better).

We step out into a patch of sunlight that is already on the run from us, chasing over the grey-green flanks of the fells. It is colder at once: I pull my coat collar up round my neck.

'Got soft, living down there, haven't you?' He laughs. He's well wrapped himself, for all that. Edna's doing. He says: 'You haven't shown up for months – when was your mother's funeral?'

Angrily, automatically, I say, 'Your wife's funeral, you mean.'

He doesn't answer. He marches up the lane between the dry stone walls. The trees are just showing the edges of the new leaves, and growth is beginning among the dried-out winter grasses. Here are a few wide flat stones jutting out of the wall. We climb up by them, over into the rocky field. His walk is the fellman's, a long strong stride. I keep up with him in spite of his jibes.

He says, 'Karin, she wasn't my wife any more. She didn't want to be.' A pause, then, harshly: 'She didn't need me. She didn't like people at all.'

'She loved me.'

'In her own way. Peter – not so much. He'd have been better off staying with me, but they all said brother and sister should be kept together. He'd never have had that breakdown if things had been different.'

'It's easy to say that.' I shut my mouth hard, to keep the rest in. And he asks, 'Did you come up here to quarrel with me?'

'No.'

It's his house: he designed it, made it conform to its surroundings, grey stone on a stone-strewn hillside, flanked by Scots pines whose trunks fire up red in the sunset. He made a good job of it. It's the sort of house that ought to be there. Here he brought Edna, away from the old terrace in Kendal with the office downstairs and its memories of my mother.

He stops by the gate.

'Do you still think it really was an accident?'

'Of course.' I'm angry again. 'Anna would never have wanted the people in the other cars to die. She pulled out without looking. She was tired. She hadn't slept.'

What right have I, in the end, to call Edna a collaborator, knowing what I know about Anna's exhaustion that morning? And yet I begged her to stay another night. I don't want to think about it. I'm too tired.

I ask him, 'How much work have you nowadays?'

'Just what I want to do. I've got a restoration job near Keswick. National Trust property. Nice.' He pauses, then says, 'Strange, all the same, when you think about it, how many of your mother's generation of painters had violent deaths. Especially the ones who came out of Germany.'

He looks at me, but I keep staring at the far peaks: they are sallow-gold against the pale evening sky and the nearer shadowed hills. He puts his hand to the latch of the grey gate.

He resents her, of course. She left him and found success: she even made money out of it. While he remained a country architect-cum-builder, converting barns and restoring old properties. It was what he wanted, and was good at, and if he'd married Edna first, he might have been content.

I eat under the surveillance of my grandmother (died 1968), my grandfather (died 1935) and my uncle (shot down in November 1943, mourned with red poppies). They stare at me out of the frames. I am subdued, and say the right things. I even agree to go to church with them on Sunday.

'You'll stay for lunch before you catch the train.'

Today is Friday; I have the whole of Saturday ahead of me. I hope it doesn't rain.

Dad says, 'The cottages I told you about, the ones I'm working on – we could go to see them tomorrow. We could have lunch out if you like – it'd be easier than coming back.'

My father shows me the cottages. On Saturday morning there is no-one else there. His fingers taste the texture of the stone; he explains how you integrate the new stone with the old. He shows me photographs of the buildings disintegrating, and his own drawings for the restoration. He talks of wood, of window-frames, doors and floorboards. I empathise with his passion. I look at his moving sensitive fingers and there all at once is the memory of Bernt's hands on my naked skin. I'm frightened. Is this a warning? Can you select what you dig out of the past?

My father's hands are long, thin, sensitive, slightly ingrained with the soil of his garden. I mustn't think of those broader hands with the springing black hairs – no! Dad's hands showed me the wild country, pulled me back from dangers, and yet demonstrated their wonder: 'Look, there's an adder, you must always make the ground shake so they feel you coming, and watch your feet, but see the patterns on his back?' They were delicate, tender, in the stream round the trout he tickled: 'Look, you get them under him, and keep them moving, ever so gently, you never let up, just keep them moving all the time, if you have to speak, keep your voice down like I'm doing and no sudden movements; you don't want to startle him.' Lover's hands under the delicate soft fish-belly, till he grabbed, pulling the fish out of the water, and thumped its head hard, on a stone: 'Kill him quickly, so he doesn't struggle.' And it was I, surprising myself, who caught a trout, while Peter sulked empty-handed.

'There's a nice pub near here where we could go for lunch.'

My legs ache from standing.

The rain is beating on the windows outside; the small pub lounge seems to shrink in on us, becomes fuggier. There is a smell of beer and bodies, a little puddle of beer on the table in front of us. I fiddle with it, pulling it out into patterns on the shiny wood of the table, and Dad, I'm sure, is irritated (though he says nothing), for which reason I carry on longer than I would have done. My hands are shaped just like his, though not so thin. They too are slightly soiled and roughened from the garden, and they move on my guitar as his did on the stone.

And he says, 'I've got a picture of your mother's you can have.'

'A photograph?' I ask, surprised.

'No.' He lifts his glass to his mouth, avoiding my eye. 'A painting.'

The barmaid shouts, 'Two ploughmans over there!' I start to get up, but she brings them over when she sees me. While Dad talks on, uncomfortably.

'Well, you can see it's awkward for me to hang onto it, and I wouldn't like to sell it, but Edna found it the other day, and – you must understand how difficult it was – I didn't really want to get rid of it, but – anyway, I think it'd be best if you had it.'

'The one she did of you. When you first met.'

The Tommies bought them, so she painted them, from photographs or from life. The family needed the food. Later she shuddered at the thought of them.

With the nearest approach to sentiment I have ever seen in him, Dad says; 'I gave her as many cigarettes as she wanted for it, because she was so pretty.' His face changes, looking me in the eye now, he says, 'You blame me still, God knows why. You've no idea what it was like for me.' I keep my mouth shut, but that doesn't put him off. 'For one thing, the situation between your grandmothers.'

'It wasn't between them. Omi never bore Granny any ill-will at all.'

'She wouldn't see your Gran, would she? And then she used to wander round the house clutching a crucifix and in those strange clothes.'

'It was quite simple, she'd dedicated herself to prayer and poverty. You're supposed to be religious, Dad, you ought to understand.'

'There's a difference between religion and religious mania.'

'And you're qualified to judge.'

'Would any convent have taken her? She was mentally ill.'

'So what should she have done? Quietly committed suicide?'

'Your mother should have left her where she was until they'd completed her treatment.'

'That place was a bin, no more, and the treatment was punishment for being miserable. Was it your God who put her there?'

But I know my father's God, and rejected him years ago. He's a patriarch who likes people neat and tidy and in their proper places. He's respectable and easily shocked, and violent with it, and he's always in the pay of the authorities.

Dad doesn't answer my taunt. He's more preoccupied with what's going on in his own head.

'Then there was your uncle.' I stiffen. 'On one side I had Granny saying your mother's people had murdered him, and on the other your mother calling him a murderer.'

Bitterly, involuntarily, I ask; 'And don't you think Anna was right?'

Dad says, 'I've killed Germans too, Karin. Plenty of them, and I don't regret it. It had to happen, and you wouldn't be here if I hadn't.'

Very true. Indisputable and utterly nauseating. The so-called French bread sticks to my tongue and I can't shift it.

14

I'm snarled up in a familiar tangle of pain, rage, and hopelessness. I gulp at my cider, and the bread swims lumpily down into my throat. It's pointless to argue, I know, and yet I say, 'You killed soldiers. He killed women and children, indiscriminately. Innocent non-combatants.'

'Not so innocent, Karin. They were steeped in Nazism, every one of them. You'll just have to accept that sometimes it's necessary to take lives in order to save lives.'

And he makes me feel disreputable in my defiance, I can feel the chip he sees on my shoulder, oh yes, so many times I've been here.

Weary at me, half-resigned to me (I've always been difficult), he asks, 'Why don't you want to be British, Karin? You were born here, weren't you? What's the point of it?' He hesitates. What's waiting to be said? Out it comes: 'You look like your grandmother; I hope you haven't taken after her in other ways.'

No, I won't have this, I won't have him make me the victim of his own grief, his own loss, his own bewilderment, so he can despise them in me and retain the myth of his own rationality. The game is too hackneyed, too destructive; whatever happens, I am made to feel guilty. I can think of no answer, and maybe it's better to say nothing, and eat my lunch, stifling the nausea.

He suggests we talk about something else. It's all I can do, short of leaving right away, and I came to do my duty after all. I can see the rest of the weekend quite clearly: we'll be careful (now it's too late) to say the right things, Dad will ask after the children (in whom he's not really interested), I will admire Edna's ornaments, and talk about gardening with Dad. Tomorrow I shall put on a skirt and go to church. There I shall repeat the prayers, though they seem to have been written with only men in mind – I don't know why they let women in the building – and my eyes will slip to the altar, where the suffering Christ is guarded, as ever, by the military. Crusaders lie cross-legged beside him, and at the back, where the children are baptised (though neither Peter nor myself,

15

who were christened Catholics) there are regimental flags. The walls are lined with monuments to the dead in battle, among them my Uncle Robert, who was shot down over Berlin as he dropped yet more bombs on the flaming city. Greater love hath no man (it says underneath) than that he lay down his life for his friend.

3

I have all the photographs; Peter didn't want them. So many times I've shown them to the children: 'Here is Anna, here is your great-grandmother when she was a little girl, with her own family – these are her elder brothers, who were all three killed in the First World War, and the two sisters who died of galloping consumption, and your great-great-grandmother, who died of the same thing, and this is Monika, your great-great-aunt who lived. This is your great-great-grandfather, with the beard. Your great-great-grandmother died a year after this photograph was taken.'

The children, amazed at so many greats, wonder at the clothes, reassure themselves I shan't die of galloping consumption, listen to an anecdote, then Elisabeth says, 'Come on,' to Sally, and they're off.

I have also the voices I can recall as if it were a tape I'd switched on, those of Helene and her sister Monika, both of whom, at different times, told me the story of their childhood.

Helene had nightmares almost every night; it had been happening since she was tiny, and she was terrified of the dark. Mama would have let her have a light, but Papa wanted her to be brave. Her sister Monika said that Lenchen, as they called her, was terribly thin, and caught every illness she had time to fit in. She had enormous green-gold eyes and a fearful smile – I can see it. She used to wake

Monika up in the night with nightmares, and sometimes Monika was angry with her.

I was seventeen before Helene told me how she woke in the dark, her body tense with fear, and there was thunder: God was angry. (That was what she told Peter and me when we were small, and the three of us trembled together.) But maybe that night it was only the noise of the steelworks in the town. In the silence that followed the rumbles she thought she could hear Mama's labouring breath. And she wanted to be with Mama: she hadn't seen her for days. Monika was fast asleep, and she didn't want Monika's capricious kindness, so she climbed out of bed and set off into the dark house, putting her small bare feet down on chilly floors, looking for the dim light round the frame of Mama's bedroom door, towards the strained loud breaths that began to frighten her more than the deeps of darkness on either side.

She opened the door mouse-quietly, and looked in. There was Mama in the bed, and there were her aunt from Breslau and Papa whose stern, frightening eyes were looking at Mama with her struggling white face. Papa was saying, 'It's the will of God. It's the will of God.' Mama's breath came shorter each time he said it, and Lenchen thought: he's pushing the air out of her chest. Why is he doing that? Then the aunt caught sight of her, shivering in her nightdress, and she exclaimed, and Papa looked, saw her, and was angry.

'What are you doing here? What does this mean? Can't you see your mother is ill?'

He himself took hold of Lenchen with his big frightening hands, carried her back to her room and dumped her down beside Monika, commanding her to go back to sleep at once, did she hear him? She shrank crying under the bedclothes and was ashamed of herself. In the morning, she wondered if it had been her fault, when they told her Mama was dead.

'You know,' said Monika, 'sometimes, after that, she dreamed Papa was killing Mama. She never told you that? I'm not surprised. Then, sometimes, she'd stare at him. How? as if she was blaming him for something. If he saw her at it he'd be furious. She never did anything he could catch her out for: just that stare. Except she would sit dreaming; he didn't like that either. Those first days after she died, he seemed to be watching us all the time. I got into trouble for laughing, but that made me giggle more. He'd slipper me. You know, one of us girls had to bring him his slippers when he came in, then he used them to punish us. When the housekeeper came, he had someone else to watch. She was a foundling, very young, and he thought she was strong, until he married her – my God, how shocked they all were, the neighbours, the family, what did they expect? The minute he got her into his bed, she began to wilt. He must have made her pregnant the first night, you could almost see the energy drain out of her. She did her duty by us, that was all. We were all lonely, but Lenchen especially, I think.'

There was the story Omi often told me, how she was a little girl looking for her sister and brothers, till the maid told her they'd all gone skating. She ran to where the skates were kept, but there were only two left skates lying there, and she took those. Of course she couldn't skate on them, she kept falling over till Monika took pity on her and lent her one of her own. While Helene skated, Monika sat on the bank and laughed with the boys. She had brown hair, I was told, curly like mine, but her eyes were the same green-gold as Helene's. Only Monika's eyes weren't fearful.

Monika said; 'I was the one who was always in trouble for cheek, but she was the one who felt sinful. She used to wake up screaming that the Devil was there – she said he had fiery eyes and was suffocating her with his black hands. She took to keeping her rosary under her pillow, so she could find it in the dark. I was glad I wasn't like her, but when she was thirteen and her hair turned bright chestnut, I was jealous. Papa thought it was terrible, and he made her life a misery telling her so.'

She said they hoped something would happen to distract him, and the war came along; that put him in a good mood. He said all the complacency and dull materialism were going

18

to burn up like paper and out of the flames would come Germany reborn. He stood (said Helene) beaming with pride and pleasure to see his sons leave for the Western Front, and they, equally thrilled, waved and shouted from out of the wagons.

'Well,' said Monika, 'you know what happened. Your grandfather was one of the lucky ones. He began as a Lieutenant – from the Reserve – and finished up as a Major with an Iron Cross to gather dust. My brothers – you know, I always think of them when I see the flies smashing on the car windscreen, in summer. And little by little, the optimism trickled away, at first we hardly noticed it, and then as time went on and food got short and the telegrams started to come –'

Helene was dressed in black, standing in the photographer's atelier beside Monika, her hair rich-coloured, belying the mourning, and Papa looked askance at her as the flash went off. The stepmother held her baby resignedly; it was a boy, Michael. Two-year-old Gustav and four-year-old Hanna huddled against her black skirt, while Karl, at five, was a man and had to stand in front of his father. The family had shrunk; all three elder boys killed within eighteen months of the war's beginning. Helene was fourteen and a half, and still at school, a clever child whose flair for mathematics didn't interest her father; that was to change, later on. Monika was sixteen, and a woman, boldly attractive.

'Papa did his best to lock me up,' she said, 'if he heard any officers were coming home on leave. He didn't think I'd stoop beneath my station, which was convenient.' My great-aunt lit a cigar, inhaled, and let smoke and laughter out of her mouth together.

'Most of the time it was knitting, making bandages, wiping the little ones' noses and bottoms, doing young-lady-like tasks about the house, and keeping out of Papa's way. Oh no, he hadn't gone to the Front, too old, too important in the steel industry.'

She fell silent, thinking, holding the cigar in front of her.

Then she said, 'She felt it so much, and there was nothing she could do. She used to go to church to light candles for them all, and for our mother. I remember once when I went with her. It was really dark, just the candle flames shaking and wobbling, making a haze round them, the way they do, and then a shadow moved in the aisle. I wanted to run away, but she wouldn't let me. She said, "Don't move. Don't make a sound. You mustn't." I obeyed her, we stood like statues, and it was the priest.'

'When she was sixteen, she told Papa she wanted to be a nurse. My God, you can't imagine the rage he flew into! I don't know why he was so determined to think the worst of her, unless he was really afraid of her – you know, he was a pantaloon, and she took him for the Lord God Almighty. You could hear him shouting all over the house: "You want to wash naked young men – that's it, isn't it? Answer me!" Of course, she didn't. She crept off to fetch him his slippers instead.'

All the same, something must have got through to him, because he decided to set both girls to work in his office. Monika had to learn to use a typewriter, but Helene went into the accounts department. She learned really fast. That's hardly surprising to me: she used to help me with my maths homework. Monika said, 'She was confident, laughing, enjoying herself. Even when the priest preached a sermon against women working – they were everywhere by then, you know, delivering the post, on the farms, in the factories – she wasn't troubled. She'd lost interest in church.'

When the war ended she was seventeen. She said even though it was too late for her brothers, she was relieved. But her father sat at the table and refused to talk to anyone. The priest, in church, inveighed against the new Republic and called it a triumph of godlessness and the work of Jews. Monika laughed, said they were fools, and offered a furtive cigarette to Helene, who tried it and was sick.

She had a few freckles on her clear skin, they look pretty to me, but the stepmother said it was a pity, with so few men left for her to marry. And she was sorry, for she would have liked to have children, but she wished you could have them without a man to frighten and dominate you. She told me that, and then said she made a great mistake: she ought to have been a nun.

She said, when the men came back from the war, so many of them had lost arms, or legs, or both, or they couldn't breathe properly, but all of them were scarred inside and out, bitter, and they felt dangerous. She didn't recognise the boys she once knew. She learnt to smoke and laugh because she felt safer if she was doing as everyone else did. She even persuaded herself she was happy.

They selected the stories they told me, and I interpret them to myself. But I feel I know the insecure little girl. At sixty she told me she felt more like that child than anyone could imagine, and she brought Lenchen to comfort me with her shared experience of fear in the dark, when I'd run crying to her room. Karin the child huddled up to Lenchen the child, to the old brittle body that still surprised its owner.

Donald says, 'I enjoyed myself with them.'

He sounds surprised and proud; he has achieved something tremendous, well done, Donald. And now, of course, he's looking at me with those dark, thick-lashed eyes and that little-boy pout and I know what he wants. The fee. Two little girls kept safe and sound and happy all weekend is worth four bare legs in a bed.

Nastily, I ask, 'Did you get the grass cut?'

'No, I didn't have time.' He's amazed I should ask. 'I was too busy with them.'

Well, it happens that I'm knackered. I want to have this soup and go to sleep. I don't want to let him sweat and grunt on top of me, pretending, at the end, that I enjoyed it, or saying it didn't matter. This too is part of history. Does it ever get written down? What statistic records the number of tired women who open their legs to give the little boys what they want and keep them sweet? His eyes say: look at me, I'm adorable. You couldn't deny me, could you?

It's what I contracted to do. My grandfather divorced my grandmother for refusing, and had her locked up for good measure.

Tough luck, Donald. You can be as adorable as you like.

Peter. Again. Perhaps he's checking to see if I really went? But no, he's already rung my father. He hears we had an argument about Omi, and Anna.

'Couldn't you have left off quarrelling with him, just for once?'

'He brought the subject up. If he abuses Omi, do you expect me to join in?'

'For pity's sake, Karin, he's an old man.'

'And that means he can say what he likes? He never extended much tolerance towards Omi because *she* was old. Anyway, we only had two arguments, and the rest of the time –'

'Well, that was two too many. What was the point of going up there in the first place?'

I'm getting angry. 'I'm not answerable to you, Peter.'

'You don't love him.'

'Don't I? Well, you know best.'

'Poor Dad.' (We ought to have some melancholic violin music in the background; surely British Telecom could arrange it?)

'Edna was always second-best, you know. He was obsessed with Anna, he still is, though he'd never admit it, and she didn't care. She only married him to get out of Germany.'

Shall I slam the phone down? No, why should I participate in these cheap dramatics? I know this is rubbish. Anna was a difficult woman to know, so apt to stare into the distance and see nothing but the shapes inside her own head, while Peter and I scrapped, and Omi prayed. But I knew her absolute integrity; she might have sold production-line portraits to keep herself alive, but she would never have sold herself like that. I tell Peter so. He snorts. I invent an appointment to get me off the phone; he wants to keep talking, but I can hear a customer's footsteps, and he won't want anyone listening.

But she did compromise herself with the paintings, so why not with the marriage? An artist needs quiet and space, neither of which Germany had much of in 1946, and perhaps she thought Dad would give them to her.

Dad was right about one thing. Her real need was to be alone. If her mother hadn't been there to look after Peter and me, we might have destroyed her. She needed acres of inner space, and even as things were, we intruded on it.

Donald wants to see what I'm reading.

'Hitler. Now why?'

'Why not?' And why do I have to sound so defensive?

'Well, apart from the excesses and the warmongering, he had some sound ideas.'

Donald. This is Donald saying this, who is British, when it's the British who've always been so self-righteous to me about Nazism. I'm angry, not only for Anna and Helene, but for Erich, my grandfather, of all people.

'Yes, his thugs beat my grandfather up and kept him in prison for two months because they didn't like his mathematics.'

He's standing there, exuding confidence, smiling at me.

'No, listen, Karin, I really feel the time has come to reassess Hitler. Now hostility has faded a bit, we can be more objective. Especially now, when all the creative political ideas are coming from the Right.'

He used to say he was apolitical, which suited me, for the contrast with Bernt. He never showed a scrap of anti-German feeling. No, stop, Karin. This is Donald playing games. I should know by now.

Serenely, he says, 'Karin, we ought to talk. It's really time you began to think about going back to work, isn't it?'

'I'm not ready yet.'

'Listen, Karin, it'll be all right, you know. You've got your D.Phil., you can get tutoring work through your college, and ease your way back into academic life. All you need is confidence.'

'Donald, I've changed. I don't want to be an academic.'

He looks puzzled. It seems it's never occurred to him that any thought in my head could be alien to any thought in his. Well, we were content, for thirteen and a half years.

Anna's done it. This is her legacy, she's wrecked my marriage, and wilted the roses over the door. She's invaded me and poisoned my feelings towards Donald. It's her revenge because I achieved the thing she didn't manage. I wasn't an artist; my guitar playing, however good, was amateur; I was forever on the outside of her studio door, and I couldn't outrage her by sleeping around, because she had a lover, Dan. The conventional marriage shocked her more than anything else, and it suited me that she didn't get on with Donald. And now she's dead – oh God, not that. Not that repeating pattern. I don't want to put Elisabeth and Sally through that.

'Well,' he asks dubiously, 'have you any ideas about what you'd like to do?'

'I want to be a medical herbalist.'

The sentence jumped into my mind, and I know it's right.

'But Karin. All the effective therapeutic agents have been isolated years ago. They can all be produced synthetically. Do you see yourself as some kind of wise woman?' He laughs gently.

I don't want Donald putting his straight lines and little square boxes into my mind. I don't want to be sorted out so he can feel safe.

'Yes, I'd like that. I want to find a gentler way of helping people, and give them time to talk. Especially women.'

His face changes: it seems he's taking me seriously.

'How long does it take to train?'

'I don't know. I'll have to find out.'

Viciously, he says, 'And then it'll be something else, I suppose. Of course, you can afford to fritter your time away.'

I hate him now.

4

I don't have to go looking for her: she comes to me when I'm alone, her hands hold mine as I do the mechanical tasks she did for us, ironing, cleaning, gardening. The voices accompany me when I sit down with my guitar.

'You don't like being ill, *Herzchen*,' Helene said, 'think of Michael, when he got the 'flu after the war, wrapped in blankets and we had to give him hot drinks all the time so he'd sweat the fever out. They don't do that now. It was terribly uncomfortable. He was only five, poor little boy. I loved him, he was so gentle.

'Oh yes, we all had the 'flu. Most people did. They said it was because we'd eaten so badly, during the war. A lot of people died, and the doctor was tired. He said we shouldn't expect Michael to live, but we should keep it from my stepmother because it was touch and go with her, too. I was up on my feet again, so I looked after the rest of them – I'd had it first. The doctor said I'd been ill so often I'd learned to fight illnesses, not like Monika, she was very bad, but she wasn't in danger.

'I had to keep putting hot water bottles inside Michael's blankets and he lay there so patient, it broke my heart. I hadn't prayed much, God forgive me, but I prayed then. His eyes were quite dull and his cheeks all flushed and puffy. I was frightened to leave him in case he died while I was out of the room. Then I came back and found him sweating. I knew he was safe. I was so pleased, but when I think of what he might have been spared – you can think you're doing the right thing, and it turns out wrong. I don't know.'

She said; 'And then came the inflation. You see, Germany had reparations to pay after the war, and we couldn't. The war had cost enough money as it was, and they'd taken our industrial areas. The government borrowed too much money, and the Reichsmark plummeted. That's why your grand-father put all his money into property: he thought houses were safe, and that's why he didn't have any faith in politicians. I didn't understand it at the time. All I knew was that Papa had to pay his workers twice a week, and negotiate a new wage with them every time: he hated it. Then they ran off to spend the money while it was still worth something. *Ach*, *ja*. I can remember as if it were yesterday, how I went past a shop and saw a blouse priced at a hundred marks, and in the evening it was a thousand. And almost everyone suffered, but the worst thing was the feeling of living on top of a volcano.'

Monika said, 'It was as if a wind machine had been switched on, and it blew away more than the value of the Reichsmark. One day Papa picked up his Bible, opened it, read for ten minutes, then clapped it shut and said that was it, the end of the world was coming, he'd found all the signs and it was only a matter of time. He sounded quite pleased. We didn't like the idea, but we didn't believe him anyway. He wagged a finger at us and said some people were going to get what was coming to them much sooner than he expected. Then he took himself from the spiritual to the secular, and reminded us that our dowries had gone, so God knew who was going to marry us now.'

Helene said this was different from the hunger of wartime, because they couldn't imagine an end to it. It seemed as if it would go on for ever. Monika and she had both had a trousseau – china, silver, damask, fine embroideries – they all went. And the piano and the family silver.

They all belonged to farmers by the time the currency was reformed – it's at times like those that you understand what really matters. Food. Still, there were a few people who were better off than ever before. Papa said they were Jews, and they'd engineered the whole thing, but when the Jewish shopkeeper down the road had just gassed himself with all his family –

Ironic, really.

Monika said, 'My father sat at table telling us there was no decency any more, only immorality and the cinema, but what could you expect from a nation that had chased away its Kaiser? I tried not to look at Lenchen, because he might guess we'd been to the cinema together; it was dark inside, after all, and we made sure no-one saw us going in. It was fun – some melodrama with ice and savage dogs and a beautiful girl needing to be rescued – very moral, if Papa could have seen it. Papa got so worked up he forgot where he was, and he told us stories about shameless painted whores of Babylon offering themselves to anyone who would have them, naked women dancing on stage, plays and paintings he wouldn't have believed could be shown. I caught sight of Karl – he was eleven – licking his lips. The younger ones couldn't understand, and my stepmother was pretending she didn't hear.

'He made it sound so interesting I took Lenchen on one side after the meal, and suggested we should run off to Berlin together. My father's sister Marlene was there, and by then the inflation had come to an end. I thought we'd get a job there, with our wartime experience. I thought nothing could be worse than staying here, with Papa getting crazier by the minute, and not even a chance to get married. Lenchen agreed. Her face lit up – she was the girl she'd been when she was working. She really wanted to get away from him. We didn't take a lot of luggage, or they'd have noticed, but Lenchen said it didn't matter: we'd get new clothes in Berlin. She loved nice clothes.'

Helene said, 'So we took the train to Berlin.' She sighed, then, almost against her will, a liveliness came into her face, and her voice started to dance. 'I remember how foggy it was, as soon as we left the lights of the station behind there was nothing but grey outside – then it turned white, then bright with the sun, till we came out of it altogether into a countryside that was strange and shiny. We hadn't been to Berlin before, and we didn't know our aunt. Papa had quarrelled with her years ago, so Monika thought she'd have us – that was wrong, of course.' This was added as a sop to the sorrowful woman she had become from the young girl who was holding the stage for a short moment. 'But she was really kind.' She stopped, and I could see her struggling. I had to wait for Monika to fill in the rest, which she did when I was living in Germany, after Helene's death.

I think that morning she didn't understand the torment she'd sown in her life. She never managed to escape from Papa, even when she was old. I'm sure it was his voice she heard in the thunder. That morning, maybe, she thought she could shed her home and her childhood like an old coat.

It was almost fifty years and many bombs later that Bernt and I hitched to Berlin – didn't I think it was a city of echoes? Some of the buildings were still pockmarked with bullets; the restored Reichstag was a monument to the flames of 1933. Among all those layers of time gone by, it was easy to find the wicked cosmopolitan city, that, even now, is one of Berlin's big attractions. In the bare-legged whores who hung out along the Ku-damm, I saw the lineal descendants of the high-booted women Helene peeked at before she turned her appalled and guilty eyes away. But she had come to the bourgeois Berlin, to one of the enormous heavy apartment blocks (the few I saw still standing were rat-baited, and a warning notice posted on the doors), ponderously decorated, street upon street, lamplit at night and full of equally heavy furniture.

Monika said; 'We'd never seen so many cars, and we had no idea how we were going to get across the roads. Helene just ran out into it, and almost got run over. I thought I'd never see her again. I felt ashamed, all the same, that she was braver than I was.'

'We laughed,' said Helene. 'Well, we were young.' Tante Marlene laughed too, when she saw them, a malicious cackle, I imagine, and, 'So you've left the old devil to stew in his own juice?' She said yes, of course they could live with her, her apartment was huge, her husband was dead, and she'd be glad of their company, as long as they could find something respectable to do with their time, and contribute to the housekeeping. She wasn't badly off, even after the inflation, her half-Jewish husband (baptised) had put enough money into property. She knew artists, musicians, and scholars – she had so many parties they didn't need to go anywhere else to meet interesting young men. I'm sure they did a good deal of laughing. It was high time.

It was Bernt who told me the next part of the story. I can feel the catch of desire in the throat: will I manage to suppress it? Too late. I'm there, in bed with him on a wet December day. We'd been making love, and though both of us had work to do we couldn't be bothered to disentangle ourselves even long enough to turn off the schmaltzy music on the radio. We lay there talking, talking. I can see his bright-eyed face with the loose black curls round it and his curling beard.

'And so you didn't know my father was illegitimate?'

'You sound really pleased about it.'

'You're not comfortable like that – let me move – is that better? I am pleased. It's the only thing that redeems my parents' terribly bourgeois lifestyle.'

The point of the story is Monika, not Bernt. But the phrasing is his: I can't get his voice out of it.

'My grandfather was a Frenchman, he was studying music in Berlin. He wanted to marry Monika; he would have brought her back to France, but she wouldn't. You know, she was years ahead of her time – she's a wonderful woman. She didn't marry him. She didn't think it'd work out, and she wasn't going to sell herself to respectability. I suppose, as far as her father was concerned, she didn't have much to lose, because he wasn't speaking to either of them at that time anyway. By the time my father Josef was born, Tante Helene was married, so she looked after him and my grandmother kept working – and soon your mother came, and those two were like brother and sister – but you know that.'

'I always thought her first husband had died. What did Tante Marlene say?'

His fingers ran gently over the more interesting parts of my

29

body: there are some memories inseparable from physical response.

'She kept my grandmother with her. She didn't care. She liked her tremendously, that's not difficult to imagine. She left her money to her, did you know that? And her apartment – for what good that did. She'd a lot put away in Switzerland – so did my grandmother, by then, but the apartment was destroyed by an incendiary in 1944, just after the old lady died.'

Then he said, 'And of course, there was no possibility of tracing my father's descent, when the Nuremburg Laws were passed. She'd deliberately lost touch with her lover – I think he was called Marc, but she had forgotten his surname. He might easily have been Jewish – she wouldn't have asked that question.' Again, there was pleasure in his voice. He had his *naïvetés*, but considering what his other grandfather was, who could think the worse of him for that fantasy?

I am thinking about Helene, who thought she'd made a successful escape. She was working in a bank, as was Monika, though only Monika was to stay there. This may have been another reason why she refused to marry Marc, that she didn't want to be snatched away from work she found interesting, to be cooped up at home. And now it comes to me how convenient Helene's marriage was for Monika. Did she encourage it? And maybe Monika's pregnancy frightened Helene, or maybe the laughter began to taste bitter, here where there were so many men without limbs or eyes or breath, and far more people to gas themselves. It could be that she saw her sister pregnant and wanted her own baby. Probably all of these, and then the fear of freedom, of herself, driving her to assimilation.

Though she met Erich at Marlene's house in Berlin, he came from the same part of Silesia as Helene. He was a pastor's son. His face was whipped by the scars of student duels, pale, faint now, they proclaimed his manliness. He had another scar you couldn't see, where a shell had slashed his chest at Ypres. He was on the small side, and quiet, but he could assert himself without making much noise.

Helene never spoke his name to me till he died, when Anna brought his wedding ring back from the funeral. She had never acknowledged the divorce, which had left her in limbo. Now, at last, stories and tears poured out of her, up till his return from Russian captivity after the war. There they cut off.

He wanted Helene; she said he was earnest and respectful. Monika said they went dancing – later, Helene wouldn't have admitted that. But she told me the romantic story of the proposal. He brought her to a café on the Kurfürstendamm, where they sat in the early evening, drinking coffee by lamplight. It was June. There was a rose on the table. He took her hand and asked her to marry him. She said yes. He supposed he'd need to ask her aunt, but she said no, her father. Then she had to explain the situation to him, and he didn't ask for his ring back, but he was pleased to hear her say she wanted her father's forgiveness. She was worried about his Lutheranism, but he said he'd agree to the children – she said he used the plural – being brought up Catholic. She said she felt safe with him. She thought he would take care of her like the tender father Papa had never been.

She might have known Papa would leave Erich's letter unanswered, and send her threats of hellfire and curses. He demanded to know if she was pregnant, and said she might as well marry, in case her soul was capable of salvation, though since she was marrying a Lutheran, he doubted it. He finished by saying he never wanted to see her again. She kept the letter among her family photographs. When she died Anna found it, showed it to me, and burned it.

She was married from Marlene's. I have the photograph. Erich looks out seriously at the camera, and his ears seem to stick out because his hair was cropped so short at the sides. He holds his top-hat awkwardly in front of him like a man who is in fancy dress and doesn't like it. Helene, in her short dropped-waist wedding dress, has her hand on her hip in what the photographer who posed her intended for a gay twenties-style gesture of insouciance, but he only succeeded in making her look unnatural.

It was Erich's doing that Anna had no sisters or brothers. Anna herself enlightened me.

'Of course they had contraception in the twenties. How do you think I came to be an only child? They used sheaths, of course – Opa insisted on it as soon as I was born. He could see how things were going, and he didn't want to bring any more children into the world. Also he wanted to save up his salary and put money into property. She would have loved to have a lot of children. That's why you meant so much to her.'

And Josef meant a lot to her, but he became a doctor, and she couldn't bear to see doctors after her last breakdown. I don't know if that was better or worse than Peter going into the RAF, certainly Josef's decision was undertaken without any of Peter's desire to hurt and shock.

It was Anna that Peter was really after. His grandmother was an incidental casualty, regrettable, but inevitable. Is it possible for me to be fair to him?

When he was talking about Dad, he was expressing his own feelings, his own frustrated, hostile love. I should be able to understand that. But he took it out on Anna. He used to barge into her studio, ignoring the closed door, till she had a lock put on.

The day he came home in his uniform he made Helene a pawn in his game, and thus finished her off. When I saw her hopeless weeping, I knew she'd given up life as well.

I can hear Dad's angry voice.

'You screwed him up, the poor lad, he wasn't even allowed to wear his uniform at home, couldn't you be proud of him the way he was?'

No. No, no, no. Never. No.

5

Donald says, 'Karin, isn't it a waste if you don't use your degrees?'

'Donald, my degrees were designed to teach me to think. I don't see how I could waste that.'

'Sally, darling,' says Donald forbearingly, 'you're getting butter all over the tablecloth.' Equally forbearingly, to me: 'But are you really thinking at the moment?'

This is how he used to keep me in order, and I read it as love.

Elisabeth and Sally are giggling and whispering about something. Sally takes offence, wails, and walks into a corner, where she stands with her face to the wall. Elisabeth tells Sally not to get her knickers in a twist. Donald, outraged, wants to know where she learned this expression.

Elisabeth says, 'Mum taught me it. Sorry to shock you, Dad.'

I think Donald would like to send me to my room.

'The things you say in front of the children!'

I've got to laugh. He's offended. I tell him not to be so tight-arsed. He goes out of the room and slams the door. I'm in disgrace. What the hell. I've had enough of his attempts to make our home what his childhood home wasn't. Elisabeth is ten, and if he thinks she learns worse things at home than she does at school, he's not half as realistic as he prides himself.

We like it better when he's away, that's the really shocking realisation. We form an easy women's club, and do and say what we like. Yes, I relax when he leaves the house in the morning.

My father said once, 'You'd better watch out he doesn't trade you in for a newer model.' I have this feeling he has a woman in America – though I've never found any evidence.

Nor have I looked for it. But when I told him, 'If ever you do it with anyone else, I hope you'll take precautions, with Aids about,' his face was like a little boy's whose indulgent mother has caught him stealing jam. I didn't probe.

I didn't care. Why didn't I care?

Meg wouldn't have noticed if he'd eaten ten jars of jam at one go; that's part of his trouble.

Will he want to remain at loggerheads all evening, to make it up in bed? It's happened before. Only this is the first time I've chosen to recognise the strategy. Sex has remained pleasurable. I've managed to keep it separate from the rest. But if that's what he's capable of, I don't want him sticking it in me. Not now.

Anna had a friend in England who was one of my grand-father's students before the war. I met her at the funeral. She is Jewish and left Germany some time between 1933 and 1939. I'll write to her and ask if we can meet to talk. She lives in Henley, so I can easily do it in a school day.

Here's Donald, tall, dark, beautiful, slim, well-groomed, apologetic. I'm disarmed.

'I'm sorry I said you were tight-arsed.' Oh God, I'm going to giggle.

Now here I am, sat down in a chair by Donald, himself on the floor at my feet, leaning his head against my knee, not groping me at all, saying oh so softly how hurt he is that I've turned hard all of a sudden when I used to be so loving and supportive. I see an opening, and try to explain to him what's been going on in me – maybe we might break the barrier that has come up between us – surely it'd be worth it?

His face falls. He's not even trying to take it in. I find myself putting my hand to my head, as if to grab a thick white rope of hair forever coming down like the White Queen's. I under-stand the play now. I've been cast as Meg.

Who never listened to Donald – or so he says. Who was the performer when it should have been Donald, when she should have been idolising him and washing his socks she was in Mexico, or at a conference in Stockholm, and sometimes she'd be gone before anyone told Donald she was leaving. I love and admire Meg, but I agreed with Donald I didn't want our children brought up that way. I didn't realise it was only the gender of the fly-by-night he objected to, and now I find myself forgetting to tell the children he's in New York, and won't be back for a fortnight. Meg didn't ever like him, Donald mourned. Does he really like our daughters?

What is he saying? A lot on his mind recently? I ask him what and he says he can't tell me. He's helping the American part of his firm to do some important research for the US government, and he's already said too much.

I stare down at the dark head. What's he doing that's so secret? He's a microbiologist. He's done a lot of work on bacteria. God. Surely not. I don't want to think it.

He turns and looks up at me, begging for unconditional, uncritical support, the poor little lost boy who is the director of a growing company with the Queen's Award for Export Achievement.

If you think the world is too insecure for children, you ought to have none at all. One baby makes you vulnerable for ever. Didn't Erich know that? And what are you saying to your one child when you think existence would be such a terrible burden for any other? Not that my grandfather hadn't read the political signs with appalling accuracy. Except that he made an error when he thought houses were safe. And another when he left politics to the people he despised so much.

They lived nine married years in the Weimar Republic; nine years in the course of which Erich built up his reputation and worked and argued with eminent physicists, many of them Jews. Helene drew me an idealistic scholar whom I could never connect with the man I knew: instead I see an arrogant intellectual who liked to feel the sharpness of his mental teeth. Who was glad to have married a wife numerate enough to have some idea of what he was doing, but not well-educated enough to compete. Because Erich had to dominate. He was dogged enough to pursue the truth he was after in spite of disapproval – he was, after all, joining those who were smashing whatever certainties were left, proving that even the material world was far from solid, was whizzing and humming with motion, even the solidest table was dancing while you ate your dinner from it. Impossible to believe and easy to dismiss, like all the other disgusting ideas and the sexual perversity dressed up as art, and the loss of faith. And so on. I know the refrain.

He had moods and glooms; she had to cheer him out of them.

'Come on. Erich, we'll go to the concert. I've got tickets for tonight.' Or she would play to him on the upright piano I have now. The work he was doing was so important!

He bought flats to rent out, and they afforded a good apartment in Charlottenburg, far away from rat-infested tenements full of war cripples and tuberculous children. Helene bought herself elegant clothes – in moderation. She was enchanting in those days, with her shy, mischievous smile, the dimples beside it, her cream-skinned, heart-shaped face and her hair with the shining red lights.

Only there must have been the unsatisfied pain of wanting another baby, the empty arms, the empty womb, the dry breasts that remembered the pleasure of suckling. I felt the same pain. How ever many times Elisabeth got me up at night. Once, Anna told me, Helene thought she was pregnant. Had one of the sheaths failed? Did she suffer a miscarriage, and did she have to endure Erich's satisfaction? She was too honest to tamper with the sheaths. Or did she suffer the sterility because she thought she deserved it? Did she read her father's letter, again and again?

Anna was blonde and blue-eyed like her father, with her father's clear-cut features. She was clever and precocious, and from the moment she made her first wavery lines on paper her drawings were interesting. She was forever on the floor, her bottom in the air, concentrating.

'What are you drawing, Anna?'

'A pattern. Colours. Shapes.'

Anna also had tantrums. She was temperamental enough to rouse plump, placid Josef and make him fight with her. Helene must have wanted to keep her arms round them to hold them secure, but she couldn't control what was going on outside, even in Charlottenburg. Far away in Wall Street, Germany's new prosperity was carelessly broken. Having been more fragile than other countries', its ruin was worse. What could they have done about that? The queues lengthened outside the pawnshops, the beggars multiplied on the streets. People came to Berlin in a hopeless search for work, and built heartbreakingly well-ordered shanty towns outside the city. The Communists marched, and Dr Goebbels mobilised the Nazis in Berlin. When the groups clashed, people got killed. One of Anna's early memories was of her mother and the maid stuffing the windows with quilts to keep stray bullets out. What else could they do but block up the window? It was dangerous to get involved.

Tightly rolled and stowed somewhere at the corner of her mind, there was the memory of the Church she was neglecting. She never lost her faith, but she didn't go to confession. She was afraid, she said, to tell the priest about her father. She had Anna baptised, of course, she sent her to the nuns to school, she took her to Mass from time to time, but she didn't ever take the Host herself. On Sunday mornings, she was often too tired, or had a headache.

She didn't like to talk about what was happening. She felt if she didn't notice it, it wouldn't be real. And yet there was the maid, saying, 'It's a lovely day. A day like today, you know why God made the world. So, potatoes, you say? Nice waxy ones, this hot weather, potato salad would be a nice thing to have, Frau Doktor, I agree with you. But I think I'll just go round the corner today, because the streets are full of brownshirts, and you don't know what will happen, do you? Na, bad times.'

Donald lifts the duvet on his side of the bed and flops in.

'Thank God it's Friday.'

'Yes.'

I'm thinking about Helene's maid. She was a survivor, and when Hitler came to power she shouted with the rest of them.

'Karin.' His voice is so confident I know he's unsure of himself.

'Yes?' I wrap my hands defensively round my body.

'Listen, Karin, if this business of your grandmother is getting to you so much – don't you think you need professional help?'

I feel he means this kindly, but I'd as soon go to a professional murderer. I try, once more, to explain why, but he backs away from the topic as if it were a snake he'd roused. A minute later, he takes my hands off my sides and begins to caress me. I'm softening, yielding, perhaps as relieved as he is to have no more discussion. You can escape into your body as into a drug, in sex, in pregnancy and childbirth and breastfeeding, or in illness; it claims you with such authority and this is one of those times of the month –

And then he bolts on me, floods me before I've a chance to get going, and, to add insult to injury, lies on top of me, sighing how good it's been. Still, this is something he's usually prepared to do something about.

'Donald, I'm not there yet. Could you help me?'

He rolls off me, and turns to face me. Quite gently, he explains that I shouldn't expect that of him. He is tired, he says, of covering up my inadequacies. If he came too soon for me, that was my fault. I should cultivate the skill to bring him when I want him. He won't let me speak, he's getting warmed up, flushed and damp with pleasure while I lie on my rocky bed of shock and frustration. He says life is based on competition and everyone must look after themselves, even within a family. He shows me how the runt gets pushed away from the nipple, to be eaten by the mother, the father also eats his children when food is short, all in the interest of strengthening the genes. Nothing is done except for genetic advantage. Altruism is a myth generated by a sick society where no-one competes efficiently. Some races – even nowadays, concedes Donald, it's unfashionable to state this truth – are less competitive than others, and go to the wall. Examples: Aborigines, American Indians, north and south. And all at once his eyes look lost and sad and I can't respond to their entreaty.

I answer instead that these groups co-operated with nature, while we are apparently bent on destroying her, and ourselves as a promotional offer thrown in with the main purchase.

Reproachfully, Donald says that this is sentimental rubbish. The challenge facing technocratic man is to work with the conditions that have evolved, ignoring wails of doom of the sort I have just articulated. It will require endless cleverness, endless creativity, the wholesale manipulation of genes, the creation of artificial environments –

I say I don't fancy living in a shopping mall myself. I like the sky and the wind and the rain –

Donald carries on regardless, just where he broke off, and his eyes are still like an abandoned spaniel's. What will be required, he concludes desperately, could even be the selection of those most fit to survive.

I ask him how. He says the market is doing it already. No need for anyone here to commit tasteless acts that offend people. The Third World is politically and economically unfit, so warfare, famine, and disease are reducing the population.

Though I've seen him construct similar theories at parties, generally when he's slightly, inoffensively drunk, sparring, glass in hand, with another intelligent person of either sex – no blatant sexism in Donald – this is something different. He is pitiable – objectively I can see that – and yet I feel no impulse to comfort him. I'm scared. Do I *want* to know what this is all about?

6

Here is a letter from my mother's friend Sabine. She'd be very happy to meet me, if there's anything she can help me with. She suggests I meet her Wednesday week, at eleven, and I'm welcome to stay to lunch. If she doesn't hear from me to the contrary, she'll assume I'm coming. I'll drop her a postcard, all the same.

Sabine's house looks quite ordinary from the outside: bay-windowed, detached, roses in the front garden. Only the heavy lace curtains in the window give you a clue: inside it's full of antique furniture, Continental china and crystal, Hungarian rugs on frames instead of doors between the rooms, an Oriental carpet on the sitting room floor, crocheted tablecloths, prints of famous paintings and two small originals by my mother. Sabine sees me looking at these, and says, 'You can have those when I'm dead. I've no children of my own to leave them to. She gave them to me. She'd have wanted them to come back to you.'

The tables are piled with the books that can't find a home on the shelves.

She offers me tisane. She's been in Vienna recently, and has bought some strawberry-flavoured stuff, she hopes I'd like to try it. There are little Continental biscuits, feather-light, delicately shaped. The place is so cluttered that it's strangely restful. The rich intricacy of the surroundings, the pattern merging with pattern makes you feel there's some hope of integrating everything in the end.

Sabine asks me how I am. I catch the question and pass it

back at her. She says I look tired. I say I am. She doesn't pursue this line.

She's eleven years older than Anna. One day when she was at work they took her parents away, and she never saw them again. After the war, she discovered they went up the chimney at Auschwitz. She goes back to Germany; she forgave, at God knows what cost. And why have I come to drag among her memories?

She asks, 'And so you want to find out about your grandfather?'

I say nothing. She puts her hands in her lap and plants her feet firmly on the carpet, her bright dark eyes looking calmly at me.

'Well, he took a very courageous stand,' she says.

I find myself answering, 'He waited till the waters washed up to him, and protested when it was too late.' I hated him. I realise that now. I don't want to hear any good of him, however mean that makes me feel beside her.

She answers, 'He chose truth when his career and his liberty were at stake. Don't you know that if he'd followed the official line he'd have been a professor in no time?'

I can see myself standing in front of Opa – he was shrunken with age, but his face was still strong-boned, intimidating. I had to get up, to make a little curtsey, and to recite a poem. Theodor Storm. I had no difficulty remembering the words, but he corrected my pronunciation and threw me off-balance. Beside him, in a low-cut dress, sat Sybille (when I was older I called her Syphilis to myself, and was always excitably nervous in case I used the word to her face; Tante Sybille, I was supposed to say). Sybille was smiling, her gold tooth displayed in her fleshy, sensual face. Later, they would catch me and ask me questions about Omi: wasn't she very difficult? Didn't I think if she'd never come to live with us my parents would still be married? And Omi was at Monika's flat, crying because she knew where we had gone.

Sabine says, 'I was there, you know, when he said it.'

I look at her at once; this is what I came to hear.

'The lecture room was packed. Hitler had just come to power, and the students were divided between those who had come to support your grandfather and those who had come to heckle him. Some of them were in SA uniform – you know, the brownshirts.

'You know, the worst had already happened, and yet I kept hoping it wouldn't be. You may find this difficult to understand, but I wasn't much worried about my Jewish descent, I felt too German. It was democracy I was appalled for, and my discipline, which was under attack. They called it a "Jewish science" and yet it never occurred to me they'd throw me out of university.

'But to come back to your grandfather. He began his lecture, but the brownshirts were determined not to let him speak. They started to chant, "White Jew, White Jew." He couldn't make himself heard. And I saw people beginning to leave, trickling out one by one – the brownshirts made room for them. They were frightened. I felt frightened too, because these people weren't just bully boys any more: they were in power. Still, a few of us pressed up to the front so we could hear him. But he stopped speaking. He had tremendous dignity.'

'Oh, I know. He used it as an offensive weapon, when he was old.'

'He used it as a weapon then. He looked round at the SA students with such contempt, it did me good, and they shut up. Then he said, very clearly, "This is the day of stupidity and subjectivism. Currently fashionable theories of physics and mathematics owe less to scientific integrity than to the need to bolster the status of mobsters who are unfortunate enough to possess neither honesty nor scruples." He must have known what the consequences would be. The next thing we heard, he was in prison.'

She pours me strawberry tea; it smells carefree, like an Oxford summer, with the gold willow-tassels trailing in the patient river. I feel she's putting her anchor back down in the present. It was cruel of me to come, selfish, ruthless.

Well, what was it, his remark? Arrogance or incredible courage? Or maybe a mixture of both; whoever would do anything if they really understood what was in store for them?

I'm sitting hunched forward, tension building up in my shoulders. My back's going to end up giving me hell, and my hands are tight and cramped. I can't loosen them.

Sabine says; 'There's always a lot of pain in a divorce, and especially when the circumstances are as traumatic as they were between your grandparents, but your mother was reconciled to him, so who are you to refuse to forgive him, or see the good in him?' She stares at me, challenging me.

I can't say anything, because I don't want to express my resentment. She seems to be telling me I have no right to my own feelings. What it adds up to is: whatever pain you feel is spurious – this is nothing to do with you. I've heard it before.

So much for restfulness. She asks, 'Karin, why are you here?'

She waits a moment. Since I don't answer, she talks on.

'You know he was one of the few people who made me feel Germany hadn't completely lost her soul. It's because of people like him that I still consider myself German.' And, challenging me again, she asks; 'Do you know what happened when he was arrested?'

'Yes. Omi told me. He was expecting them when they came. They didn't leave him much dignity. They threw him on the ground and kicked him in the groin, then stamped on him a few times with their boots; shiny, gleaming boots. Then they dragged him off. He had blood on his face, so they must have aimed at his head. But I think it was later they knocked his teeth out. They wouldn't talk to Omi, or tell her where he was being taken. And Anna saw it all. She was eight.' I say this reluctantly; I'm proving her point.

And suddenly I'm saying angrily, weepily, 'Always him! Never her! He was the star, and she was the one who mopped up all the shit for him. When he'd destroyed her, he hated her for it. They sacked him. Well, didn't that affect her as well as him? When he sat in the study all day, trying to do research,

when he gave up coaching backward children because he was
too clever, when he had to report to the police every week,
don't you think he fed on her strength? Was it her fault she got
him out of prison, or should she have left him there to be a
martyr? It might have been better, how do I know? He never
measured up to that moment, never again.'

I can't accept her light, old arm round my shoulders. Who
am I to ask pity of her? And what I say oversimplifies it, as
words always must.

She says, 'You have to live through a situation before you
can judge how people behave.'

'I'm not judging him – or her. I'm judged with them. I
always have been. What can I say to you? Or a man I met
once who was one of the first soldiers into Belsen? When he
said to me there must be something especially evil about
Germans, I began to think it must be true.'

Sabine says, 'The Quakers who got me out of Germany
were Germans, you know, Karin. I went back to find them,
years later, and several of them had died in the camps. And
then, when I got engaged to an Englishman, my mother-in-
law didn't like me, because I was German, but also because I
was Jewish. Karin, in the end, it's you who are judging
yourself.' She pulls out a handkerchief and blows her nose.
Then she says, 'You're right to think it through, don't mistake
that. But it hurts me to think of you and all those other
guiltless young Germans who carry this terrible burden from
the past. And then –' A long pause while she waits for her
thoughts to fall in order. 'Personal life is askew to politics,
always, always. How many Jews wouldn't have supported
Hitler if anti-Semitism hadn't been part of his programme?'

'I'm not sure I can take that on board.'

'Why not? And for your man who went into Belsen, he was
lucky he hadn't the same choices to make. We're all caught
up in history, sometimes the stream is calm, but when there
are rapids, people get thrown about and lost, and how do you
weigh up innocence and guilt? Think about what the Russian
soldiers did to your mother, did she deserve it?'

It must be the constriction around my heart that's making it pound so hard; at moments of shock part of you can stand aside and be surprised how true the clichés are.

'What do you mean?' That's one way of fending off, for another moment, what has already arrived.

She asks, 'You didn't know?'

'My mother was raped? No, she never told me. I might have guessed, though. It happened to so many German women, didn't it? Was it only once? Please, tell me the truth.'

Again the silence. I can hear her laboured elderly breathing, hampered yet further by distress. This is too dreadful for tears, yet inside me I'm wailing to Anna: why didn't you tell me? Why did you keep it from me?

Her arm is still round my shoulders. She tightens it, and says painfully, 'She was abducted by a unit during the battle, and they kept her for a week – for their entertainment. She was freed by an officer, in the end. He took her back to your grandmother. The fighting was over by then. Your grandmother found a doctor for her.'

'Why did she need a doctor?'

'To carry out the abortion.'

I am very composed, cold, and shivering.

'Omi was a Catholic.' Was it a girl or a boy? Another half and half, like Peter and myself. But one that would have been far too much for her to cope with.

'She never hesitated.'

'And Anna never told me. She told you.'

'Only because of my parents in Auschwitz, just once, never again.'

'Omi escaped?'

'I believe so. Your mother never said she didn't.'

But would she have told? And what about my aunt Hanna, who was with them at the time? Only Josef could have told me, and he's dead. I'm left with his account that I now realise was edited, bowdlerised for my consumption. Why did they need protection against me? And Bernt, does he know?

And what did it do to Helene? The baby was dead, and it

was she who had arranged it. She did it for love. How do you choose when love and love conflict?

I say goodbye. Sabine takes me rather anxiously in her arms. It's raining. I beg her not to stand in the rain. Thank God, she's going in, so I can run through the wet, getting my hair soaked, and my face, as if I could get away. As if I could leave it all behind.

The wipers flip back and forth, never quite clearing the windscreen. I'm shut in, and the ventilation system can't clear the fug in this car. Processed air is always stale, though if Donald had been serious the other night, that's what he'd have us breathing all the time in our artificial environment. The countryside is blurred and unreal, only the ribbon of road requires attention. I'd better concentrate on my driving, then I won't have to think.

I wonder if my father knows? Surely not, if he had, he'd have understood that Anna could never have left her mother to rot in the mental hospital. She'd never have had to threaten, 'Then I go back to Germany,' when he asked what she'd do if he refused to have Helene in the house?

She let me stay out as long as I wanted when I was a teenager, but she was always working late when I got in. What did she go through, those nights I was out till two? And I think I understand the lock on her door. Oh, God, Peter. Yes, but that was why she didn't take me seriously, when he wrote that letter before his breakdown. She couldn't afford to. I always knew there were things she couldn't bear.

The road, Karin, the road. You could overtake that lorry, there's a string of cars behind you on this hill. Watch them all whip past now, what do I care? I'm not so keen to arrive.

For all my rages, I've invariably buried a lot, and it's soured the ground where I put it, sometimes worked its way up and begun to poke. Here comes the letter Peter wrote me three weeks after Omi's death – I can see the narrow-lined file paper, the black ink and scrawly handwriting that said he wanted sex with me. It took a lot of trouble to make out some of the words, and I felt unutterably filthy that I tried. The feeling grew worse when the graphic details he went into made my genitals quiver with horror, and I was frightened I might want it in spite of myself. I hadn't gone to bed with anyone, I'd been going out with Jack for six months and he hadn't wanted it either. He was kindly and reticent, my refuge from those who thought my Bohemian background made me easy, or the others who wanted the status of dating Anna's daughter. Since he had a controversial High Court judge as a father, Jack understood. And my best friend at college was Mary, daughter of a bishop famous for his die-hard stand against new liturgies and, before he died, the ordination of women.

I'd never dreamed of some of the things Peter wanted to do with me, and I wouldn't consider some of them even now. I suppose he got them out of soft-porn magazines. I don't want to remember too well.

When I took the letter down to Anna, I wasn't just playing Peter's game for him, I wanted to shake her. I was genuinely shocked and looking for comfort, but we were making each other so miserable. Neither of us could supply the other with the emotional support we used to get from Omi – we might have done if Anna had been able to share her grief, but she hugged it to her, defying me to participate. And when I said I was going to stay with my friend Mary, she accused me of abandoning her.

Flip-flap, flip-flap, the wipers go over the glass, and more rain pours down. They're just holding their own. The car feels uncertain with all the water under the wheels, for all it's a solid, reliable Volvo.

Anna said, '*Er ist übergeschnappt.*' He's gone crazy. Her face distorted, became a grotesque sketch of itself, and she began to cry.

I asked, 'What are you going to do?' That was a challenge, but she'd already taken the whole thing to herself.

'Nothing. He belongs to the RAF now. They'll have to deal

with it.' She was shaking and the tears came faster, but I couldn't put my hand on her to comfort her. Perhaps I should have done, and we might have wept together. Instead, I asked,

'What about me?'

She stared at me.

'You? You'll be all right. Nothing bad is going to happen to you.' I thought she sounded contemptuous. As an afterthought, she added, 'Don't worry.'

After that, the thought of how I'd opened my mouth to kiss Jack was disgusting. I ditched him. He didn't forgive me. I went out with other men, but only as friends. If any of them began to grope or tried to slobber in my mouth, that was it.

I should have put my arms round Anna.

More people overtaking. They shouldn't drive so fast in the rain, or take such risks. Do they think they're invulnerable?

7

The children know there's something wrong. They're clingy, reminding me that they exist and need me – and Elisabeth at ten differs from Sally at five only because the demands she makes are different. (There's a voice inside me, screaming for aloneness and quiet. But I carry on.) I chauffeur Elisabeth to her piano lesson, and listen to Sally reading. She mucks about and won't get on with it or go away. I am excessively patient because I haven't the strength to keep anger within bounds.

I'm not my own property, after all. I belong to the generations that came before and are to come. Thus Donald claimed me for marriage and a family – I came quietly. It was Hitler's theme, but that doesn't completely invalidate it. (The abortion debate sets the interests of the child against those of the mother, but supposing the interests of the mother were always at war with those of the child? Or else why couldn't Anna have told me? She was trying to protect me. Sabine said so.)

As an ironic reward for my obedience, Donald is home on time tonight – only one meal to get. (To avoid kissing him, I'd better pretend I have a cold sore coming.)

The children don't want to go to bed. Sally won't let me finish her bedtime story. I do as they require. At last they let me go. Donald goes up to them and returns to the sitting room with a newspaper. I seize my guitar. Bach. Cool, mathematical, precise. Concentration is better than sleep: there's no danger of dreams. It's finished far too soon. I'm casting about for something else to play. Donald interrupts.

'Nice.' (He doesn't mean it, he only wants to make a noise.)

Angrily, I play a few phrases, chromatic, logical, discordant. I say, 'I've found out today that my mother was captured and raped by God knows how many Russians during the Battle of Berlin.'

The penis is a policeman. It keeps women in order. If they behave themselves it can be kind and friendly, but often it deals out punishment as it thinks fit. I can see it with its blue helmet at the top of the rearing stalk.

'Who told you?'

I give the information, with the relevant details.

Donald frowns. 'She wasn't the only one. If that's what really happened.'

I snap, 'Do you think she offered herself to them?'

'I mean, how do you know that woman's telling the truth?'

'It rings true.'

'Well,' says Donald, 'it might explain quite a few things, I admit.' Is there an undertone of satisfaction in his voice? Pause. He looks at the carpet, fiddles with his newspaper, looking at me warily – and I'm not even surprised by his reaction. He won't sympathise with my baffled love, or fetch out and soothe the pain I haven't approached myself. What lies between us forbids it – there's so much we don't dare approach now, he and I.

He says, 'Karin, you seem to be making me responsible for it. I mean, think about it yourself. The way you told me, for example.'

'Jesus, Donald, do you think it was easy to tell you?' I should have held that back. There was a moment, just then, when we might have reached the heart of what lies between us, because those words belong to another occasion, the morning of her death.

He says, 'That's not the point.'

We've passed the point, that's what's happened, and whether we could find it again – perhaps all I do want to do is blame him, maybe he's right.

He says, 'It's nothing to do with me, what those Russian soldiers did to your mother – but I can tell you one thing, Karin,' – it's like an express train, if you miss your station, when the next one is so many miles off it seems unreachable, and meanwhile the train is speeding away – 'I can't understand why she made that ridiculous protest at Greenham. If we didn't have a deterrent, they'd be over here, doing the same thing.'

He's actually smiling, his expression says, you won't counter that one in a hurry. What do you say to that?

Nothing, Donald, I have nothing to say. It's easier to talk to my guitar. Anna bought it for my eighteenth birthday, and Bernt envied me its beautiful tone. And why am I remembering Bernt now, in the middle of this horror?

I won't think of Bernt. I'll think of Anna (his cousin and nominal aunt) or my children. But memories are like children, they're not always easy to silence. And Sally looks like Bernt. It's not difficult to see him at her age, the same curly black hair, only short, the same wide, dark eyes with long black lashes, rather pot-bellied as small children are – no wonder his mother, Maria, was so passionately in love with him. He was about eighteen months older than Sally, and I six months older again when Tante Maria surprised the two of us investigating each other in Monika's bathroom – why didn't we have the wit to lock the door as well as shutting it? Maria made me feel so bad I never even tried to tell her the whole thing had been his idea – 'Please, Karin, let me see you with nothing on, I need to, I'm going to be a doctor.' And I, all naïve, agreed on condition he would undress for me, because, as I was going to be a painter (what else?) I would have to draw naked people. Of course I got the blame. I'm female. I can imagine a judge (with Donald's face and voice) sternly telling Anna she brought it on herself. After all, she was asking for it, wasn't she, wandering the streets in the middle of the fighting? Get away from me, Bernt.

'Karin.' I can hear his voice, making an endearment of my name. 'Karin.'

Bernt, you softened me up for Donald. If it hadn't been for you, I might have remained free. I might have got on in the diplomatic service, as I wanted (which neither you nor Donald thought I should do).

If I hadn't decided to spend a year as an English-language assistant in a German school; if Anna hadn't persuaded me to try for Bonn, so I'd be near Monika, and Bernt could introduce me to other students; if I hadn't got a school near the university; if my landlady hadn't hiked the rent up further than I could afford, as well as slamming a tax on baths, so I spent two weeks chasing newspapers, unoccupied phone booths and free telephone lines – always to discover when I got through that the room was let; if Monika hadn't owned a small flat which she gave Bernt to spare him that misery; and if Bernt had been less kindly, less willing to let me have the sitting room to live in; if I had refused the offer and asked Anna for the extra cash. Maria could have told me – right from the beginning she knew exactly what would happen.

And there I lived, permitted to be one of the lads, which pleased me tremendously in those days, Bernt and I and Günter the beer-bellied philosophy student. Bernt had grown his black curls long, and had a beard. Maria said he had turned into a hippy, but when he smiled tenderly at her she forgot to be angry and defended him against Josef's disapproval. It was only where I was concerned that she was implacable. She sat in the flat, or at Monika's – in both of which places Josef insisted she tolerate my presence – her arm round her son, complaining affectionately because he wouldn't bring his washing home for her. He said she had enough to do as Josef's practice nurse. (He disapproved of this arrangement.) She turned from him and told us delightedly that he'd always been like this, so protective of her, had helped her in the kitchen and brought her cups of coffee when she was tired. She hardly ever talked directly to me, only sidelong, at me. She was always suspicious of Josef's friendship with my mother.

Bernt's eyes were still beautiful, but he wasn't anything like as goodlooking as Donald, who would call him short. (He was the same height as I am, about five-foot eight.) But there was a brightness about him and people were always pleased to see him. It added to the attraction that he seemed surprised and grateful to them for liking him. He was studying medicine – in the intervals between taking Western society apart so that he could decide how it worked and then criticise it. He rejected authority and idolised Rudi Dutschke. He spent hours instructing me exactly how to arrange my own life without interference, and he thought the diplomatic service was a hotbed of fascists. He hadn't been faced with conscription: they were waiting to call him up when he qualified. Günter chewed his droopy dark moustaches and said he wouldn't be allowed to do alternative service. Bernt said he wouldn't put on the uniform, and would refuse to work. I asked him what he'd do if they confronted him with someone bleeding to death? Bernt said he'd react as a person, not a doctor, which led us into a long and enjoyably cerebral argument about whether this was possible.

We used to improvise together on our guitars. I had been properly taught, so I led, and if it got too complicated for him to follow he would laugh, rest his hands on the strings, and listen to me for a while. Sometimes Günter would knock and come in with his smelly cigar and a notepad – he smoked hash in the vain hope that it would release the lid of the super-ego and let brilliant poetry well up out of his subconscious. We took the odd puff of his joint, and felt we were proving something. Bernt finished with his girlfriend.

It was December when I walked wearily home through the rain with a worsening sore throat, and flopped shivering into a kitchen chair. I sat there quite unable to move, waiting for someone to find me. It was Bernt I wanted – I can recapture the poignant delight of his arrival, his dismay at my shivers and wet clothes, and his hand on my burning forehead. He got me out of the chair and sent me to bed, where he brought me a hot water bottle. Later, when I was burning hot, he cooled my face with a wet flannel.

He was careful of my privacy, in spite of which the hairs began to sing on my skin when he came near me. He must have felt something similar, and as soon as I was better I was in his arms – and then found I couldn't open my mouth to his tongue.

I clung to him with the same feelings I used to have when stealing raisins from Edna's cupboard, because I felt I deserved this; it was the just punishment for provoking Peter's desire – and yet I couldn't let go of Bernt – and besides which, I was filching him from Maria. And then frustrating him into the bargain. God, what a poisoned cocktail. But Bernt said it didn't matter, he wanted me to be happy, and there were other things we could do. I was so relieved I burst into tears and told him what was wrong, and more. I told him what I'd told nobody else, and what I hadn't even realised myself till he gave me the time to express it.

But that was the way he was, that's why he's become a holistic doctor, committed to listening. Everyone wanted to confide in Bernt – they were sure he would accept the darkness they cringed away from and give them back to themselves whole. Sometimes what he heard threatened to overwhelm him. I wonder how he manages professionally?

His hands had a deliberate gentleness that made them the

more erotic. It wasn't long till I let his tongue in, and not long after that I pulled him down on the bed with me and brought him all the way with no contraception – we were lucky. At the time, all that worried him was hurting me. He knew he was capable of violence, and he was afraid of it.

Yet when I asked him once if he thought he was good, he hesitated, then said yes, he did, and what about me? I said no. I think I knew then I'd end up hurting him.

He liked me to be a fierce lover. If I wanted to lie passive and be pleased, it disturbed him that he liked that too. It irritated me sometimes that he was so protective of my autonomy.

We hitched to Berlin together. It was hot late August and I was on the point of going back to England. Still we talked as if nothing was ever going to come to an end. The crescent moon hung in the sky like a thin section of ripe apricot and we swam naked in the dark Wannsee, and made love on the beach afterwards. Out there, as we read in the newspaper the next day, a man was trying to escape to the West by swimming the same water, only to be shot dead by East German border guards – maybe while Bernt was saying, 'No, listen, Karin, all this smartness and tidiness that you like about Germany, I wish I could make you see it doesn't matter how a shop window is arranged, what it's about is extortion – worse, a shiny coating for poison underneath, yes, poison. We had a restoration after the war, no revolution, and the whole system is riddled with Nazis. Look at my grandfather, out of prison and into the bureaucracy –'

I said, 'It does matter, it has to matter. How would it improve anything if the streets were full of rubbish the way they are in England?'

'They ought to be full of shit, that's what would be the honest thing, and blood, too, we ought to have to wade through blood, the money this country has made out of Vietnam.'

We went to Charlottenburg, and looked at the house where Anna was born, where she and Josef played like sister and brother, and the hairs rose on the back of my neck. I felt like a puppet dancing to someone else's tune. When Bernt tried to kiss me, I pushed him away. I said, 'Your mother hates me.'

He said, 'She's jealous.'

I was really angry. 'I don't want her to be jealous. I'm not Anna, you're not your father. I want her to love me. I can't bear it that she hates me. She stops me existing, can't you see that?'

He couldn't. I accused him of keeping Maria like a little savage cat, content that she bite everyone else and purr in his lap. He wouldn't answer. My head began to ache, and got worse all the way round the art gallery we'd gone to for my pleasure. We went back to Günter's sister's flat – she was in Greece, wasn't she? – and he massaged my head and neck and shoulders, which usually worked magic, but that night it made the pain worse.

Donald made it all seem so unreal, such an ephemeral relationship with no solid words like marriage or children or house or insurance. I met Meg and we fell in love with each other. Maria made me feel like the Other Woman. I was sick of myself, half-despised Bernt's care for me, wanted to lose myself and be transformed as Wife, Mother. Bernt wouldn't have married me, and I didn't want to live like Anna. I can go round like this, in circles, and it doesn't finish the business.

He sends me a word-processed Christmas letter, standard issue, personalised because the machine knows how to insert Liebe Karin at the beginning. The letter comes like an annual reminder that I had the right to do as I would. I know therefore that he has an open relationship with a woman called Ulrike – a lecturer in sociology – that he's followed the predictable path, peace movement, Green Party. And he did refuse to work as an army doctor when they told him his objections were frivolous; being a doctor was being a doctor, wasn't it, never mind the uniform? Bernt refused to put the uniform on, and they locked him up three times before they reviewed his case and let him do alternative service after all. Josef, in London on his own to visit Anna, was half proud of his son, half convinced Bernt had made a fuss about nothing. Three months later Josef was dead of heart disease, and Anna told me he'd come to say goodbye.

I send Bernt a Christmas card. I signed Anna's letter to him after Josef's death, but I've never answered the letter he wrote me after Anna was killed.

I've got a headache. I can't breathe easily, and my heart is pounding. I'm confused, accused, culpable and cruel. And Anna never told me, why?

8

Sally's face is fierce and serious, frowning into the distance, her pansy-dark eyes crumpled round the edges. Her grubby small fingers stub down on the strings and crook on the bow of her friend's violin. She says she has to learn. She seems to know how to hold it, how to put the bow across.

It's Anna's expression, composed, almost fanatical, entirely attentive to what was within her – catching at the ragged edge of what might be a memory or a dream, I can see her in Granny Birkett's sitting room, observing her mother-in-law, God knows what process going on in her head, ignoring Granny's unnerved chatter. Then I see her turn to my father, and say, 'Alan, I've got a job at an art school in London. I'm going next month. I think it's time we parted, don't you? I can't work here any more.'

Of course I'll ring Gail and find out if she can teach Sally. I couldn't frustrate the child. Even though the image persists: a woman stands up and leaves the room, kicks away the break-neck mat in the corridor, opens the front door, shuts it carefully behind her and walks away from her family through the pouring rain. Her face is indistinct now, she could be anyone.

Donald is shaking me. He says I have to wake up. Don't I

know what time it is? My eyes are heavy. I can't see the clock. I suppose I'd better get up but I feel so desperately tired. I'd like to sleep for ever.

What am I doing on the floor? Donald is crouched over me – he looks as if he was going to wet himself. I've passed out, apparently.

'Karin! What the hell do you think you're doing?'

'I didn't mean to.'

He puts his hands on me and begins to heave me upright – I'm on the bed now, I must have been away again.

He's shoving a thermometer under my tongue.

'Don't let it flop about like that! Oh God, I'd better hold it.'

It makes me feel sick, that hard poking thing – I can't stop myself retching. Donald catches the thermometer. Thirty-nine point five Centigrade. Have I any other symptoms? Moving my dull mind round my body, I can find nothing but aching legs and arms.

'It's the 'flu.'

'I'm going to ring the doctor. You feel sick, don't you?'

'No, it was the thermometer.'

'Vomiting is one of the symptoms –' he stops.

'Symptoms of what?'

'Oh – look, if I'm going to get the surgery –'

'Donald, I don't want the doctor. This will pass. I want the loo, and I'll need help to get there.'

'I'd better take you, then.'

'I've got a headache.'

'Headache,' he says, like a meditative policeman at the scene of the crime. 'I'm going to ring the doctor first.'

'If you don't want to change the bed because I've wet it you'd better get me to the bathroom.'

His fingers dig into me as he supports me – my head is swimming again – he's picked me up now and is carrying me, grunting with the effort. He dumps me on the toilet seat with the edge of my nightie underneath me – I can just about pull it out before I have to let go. A stupid voice is bleating inside me:

he wasn't like this when I had the children. He was kind when I had the children. His hands were gentle when I had the children –

He wants to know why I'm crying.

This time he pinches me as he lifts me up; I've been practically dropped on the bed, and he's back in the bathroom, running hot water and scrubbing his hands. Am I so filthy?

'Donald, don't ring the doctor.'

'Don't be a fool, Karin.'

Is he shivering as he stands there by the door?

'I don't want him.'

'Karin, I've got to make sure this isn't –'

Shit. There he goes down the stairs, thumping louder than he need. He's shouting at the children to be quiet.

'Mummy's ill. No, you can't go to see her, I don't want you catching it. Now, I've a lot of phoning to do.'

I can't have the children, and I've got to have the doctor. It feels terribly lonely. Phone calls, one to the doctor, another to work, and the third?

He's coming up the stairs again, but his feet are calmer. They beat out: I'm an important busy man, unwarrantably snatched out of my normal routine – here he is.

'I've rung my mother. She's coming to look after you. You must see I couldn't possibly afford the time off, the way things are at the moment.' He sounds sulky. He is resenting 'my wife' and 'my mother' together, and the best thing is to throw them together. 'The doctor will be here about two o'clock. I'll have to go out and take the kids to school, but I hope my mother will be here before it's time to collect them, so I don't lose the whole day. She's at some kind of crank stall this morning. You'd think an intelligent woman like her would have more sense – Greenpeace or something, maybe she's worried the tapeworms are dying out. Lucky I've got something home with me, so the morning won't be completely wasted.'

I hope Meg gets here before the doctor does. If I feel ill as a bid for attention from Donald, I miscalculated my strategy.

A small black insect is crawling up and down the hills and valleys of the duvet, moving with willed optimism, for it seems to have no faith it will ever leave this wasteland. I don't think it's a cat flea, looking for substitute blood. This thing is longer. But it's not an insect at all, it's myself and herself at the same time, as can so often happen in dreams – am I asleep? I suppose so – it's a woman, dressed in her best, high staggering shoes and a black suit, and a black hat with a polka-dotted veil, going from office to office, trying to get Erich out of prison.

It feels so alone. Only Ursula from across the street, and Monika and Tante Marlene support Helene, suggest new people to try, ask about for lawyers; most of them won't touch it.

People are avoiding her now, acquaintances and friends pretending they don't see her. If they can't manage that, they've always got an urgent appointment in five minutes. The important people (if they see her) treat her like dirt, rub her face in Erich's sin (for which he has never come to court) point to the danger of Communism – haven't they just set fire to the Reichstag – the need for strong government and the irresponsibility of academic tongue-wagging which might undermine it.

She goes to confession for the first time for years. The priest has a list of sins to convict her of, before he will even listen to her main concern. She has been so negligent in her observances it's not surprising she's come to grief. God has sent her this trial to teach her to trust him. He implies it is frivolous to worry about Erich, since he is a Lutheran; moreover, says the priest, the Führer and the Holy Father have just signed a concordat, which proves the Führer's good intentions, and with the danger of godless Communism – and didn't they set fire to the Reichstag? Helene leaves the box with the Aves and psalms she has to say, her sins heavy on her head despite the absolution. Erich remains in prison.

She is walking the streets, riding trams and trains, calling at offices, giving her name, her business, agreeing to come back tomorrow, next week, in two days' time. She meets one of Erich's colleagues in the street. He is embarrassed, avoids her eyes, has to hurry home to his sick wife. She drags herself home to find Anna drawing a picture of the Führer.

Anna asks, 'Mama, what colour are the Führer's eyes?'

Red, like his hands. Will the last she sees of Erich be a registered parcel, his ashes in a cigar box? The whispers are going round, and she's sure most of them are true. Oh God, what has she said, with the maid listening?

'Mama, didn't you hear me?'

Thank God.

'Blue, Anna, blue. But you mustn't call me Mama any more, sweetheart. It's a French word. You must use the German word. You must call me Mutti, remember that.'

'Yes, Mutti.'

Anna's new obedience is a relief and a worry. The child goes back to her picture: Hitler, frighteningly well-drawn, glowers at Helene from under Anna's fingers. He's in their home, his voice coming out of the radio, now his face. The maid will put him up where he can watch them all. He knows everything Helene has ever done wrong, he is the Other appointed by God the Judge to take away the unrighteous. It's getting hot, and hotter. Are they the flames of hell or are the incendiaries falling already?

I'm awake. It's I who am hot, burning, and the duvet is far too heavy for me to move. I struggle with it, shift it at last. My mouth is dry and tastes disgusting. Can I get to the bathroom to fetch myself a drink? No; the minute I sit up I begin to fade away. This is ridiculous. I'll call Donald.

No answer. He might be out with the children. He might be in the garden. He might have decided not to answer. Omi always came, no matter what time of night, but she's somewhere else now, and she can't hear my sobs either. Please, Omi, let me dream of you.

Donald is coming to kill me.

I know it's a dream. I want to wake up, but it's looping round and again and again he's in the door, his hands ready to grip my throat –

This time it's different, the hands aren't brutal and obvious, they're moving ever so gently with the ripple of water round my throat, getting ever closer, gentle, like a lover's, right up to the moment when they close, hard and choking.

I'm awake. Thank God. I can just see the bedside clock: it's twelve, that's easy to see. My mouth is completely dry now. I couldn't call him if I wanted to. My head is pounding. I can smell my own foul breath.

I don't want Donald. I'm scared of him. When Meg comes, she'll get me some water.

I am an echo chamber. I can hear more than I can stand.

It's a nightmare. I'll soon wake up.

That's what they all think.

Listen, thunder. We must pray for forgiveness; God is angry.

This is simple faith, this path beset with traps, any one of which means damnation. (Don't bite the Host, it would bleed.) Every sin must come out at confession, and it's only now, with the body of Christ already on my tongue, that I've remembered my father. (If, when you bring your gift to the altar, you remember that anyone has anything against you –) I didn't think of him, I didn't think it was a sin – oh, save me, forgive me, I've bitten the Host. Is the metallic taste in my mouth only the sourness of fear, or is it blood, will it trickle down my chin so everyone will know – they know about me already, that's why they ignore me on the street, why I'm all on my own.

Tramp. Tramp. Tramp in my head. Marching feet. Kicking, violent, damaging boots, blood-stained. I can't bear to hear it any more. Why won't it stop? Please, turn the radio off. I don't want to hear the baying crowds, or the Führer who's caught Erich. Maybe he's already putting the cigar box in the post? I can't see properly –

Oh, God, the door. There's someone at the door. They're coming for me this time. They're coming for me. Is there anywhere I can hide?

There they are on the stairs: two pairs of businesslike male feet. It's not the Gestapo, it's Donald and the doctor. Anyway, I couldn't hide. I'm half naked: will I be able to cover myself before Donald opens the door? It's such a struggle to do anything.

I am Karin Birkett, D.Phil. I have no reason to be afraid of this doctor, who I know to be no more all-powerful than myself. The fact remains, I don't want the doctor. I want Meg.

It's Dr Fox, young, with pointy ears – but no brush at the rear. All the same, his bedside manner makes me feel like Jemima Puddleduck. Is this what Bernt has become?

He addresses me as Mrs Birkett; I croak that I am Dr Birkett. He remembers me: a difficult patient. I want him to go away.

Donald cuts in with a businesslike account of my symptoms. Dr Fox looks relieved that he can talk sensibly to someone. I am reduced to the status of a child. He takes my temperature and my pulse, speaks kindly to me. I'd like to kick his leg, or some more vulnerable part.

Dr Fox asks if I've taken anything to get the fever down. I shake my head. For the second time today, the thermometer drops out of my mouth – just let him try to reinsert it. Dr Fox says my temperature is high, so it would be a good idea. Donald looks at me reproachfully. Dr Fox brings out his cold stethoscope and puts it under my nightie. I endure it because I'm not strong enough to protest, and my mouth so dry I can hardly speak. I don't want to breathe in and out to his dictation.

Dr Fox: 'Headache?'

Myself, through dry lips: 'On and off.'

Dr Fox wants to know if my neck is stiff. I tell him it's not, but he takes my head and moves it about. I'm terrified of this: I don't trust him. Then he begins to scribble in his notes, and gives his verdict. I am convicted of calling him out unnecessarily. It's a virus, there is (of course) a lot of it about, though I've got it particularly badly. Paracetamol for the fever and keep drinking. I say I'd be glad to drink if some water was brought me. (Oh, good, Donald's embarrassed.)

Dr Fox: 'Haven't you had anything to drink all day?'

Myself: 'No. He hasn't been near me since this morning.'

Donald has nipped into the bathroom and is getting me water out of the tap, which he brings, with some paracetamol. Why is he so careful not to touch me? The tablets get stuck *en route* and sit like small millstones in my neck. I soak up the water trying to wash them down, and Donald has to get me more. Dr Fox seems uneasy – maybe he thinks he might be dragged into a marital dispute?

'I'm sure you'll be better in a few days Mrs – Dr Birkett.' No medic seems to like giving me my title, which is why I always make them do it. And his is only a courtesy title: I've seen his qualifications by the surgery entrance. I worked for mine.

Donald follows him out of the room, shutting the door, but I can hear him ask, 'You've definitely seen this elsewhere? I mean, the way she can't move –'

If he's really as anxious as he sounds, I don't understand his behaviour towards me. What does he think I've got?

Dr Fox mumbles his way out of earshot. And I can hear the doorbell again. Is it Meg? I do hope it's Meg. It might only be the meter-reader, or else it's the men with the straitjacket, except they come later.

There is a jumble of talk round the sound of opening and shutting doors. There's a woman's voice. It's Meg.

In she comes, her hair trailing untidily behind her, her jumper on back to front. She kisses me warmly, and starts pulling things out of the bag she is carrying, saying, 'Oh, you poor love, now you must just rest up and let me look after you, and you needn't worry about the house, because I'll do everything, and get the meals and take the children to school and back.' I know the kitchen will shortly look like the debris of an earthquake, and I won't be able to find anything when I'm better, but she's a wonderful cook and the children love her as much as I do. By now I am surrounded by white grapes, mineral water, a bunch of expensive flowers, an enormous bottle of eau-de-Cologne, and Meg's arms.

She says, 'There, darling, you're crying because you feel so bad, but it'll soon be better, you'll see.' Which makes me cry more, because there are so many times when I feel in need of mothering, it's heartbreaking when I get it.

Donald, who has brought up Meg's own invalid table, asks crossly, 'Can I go to work now?'

Poor, poor Donald, little baby left outside a shop in his pram by a wicked mother who had forgotten he existed – she had only just had him and she did run all the way back when Conrad, uncharacteristically observant, asked her where the baby was. A little boy living among dust and cobwebs and disorderly heaps of paper which the au pairs sometimes moved from one side of the room to another; whose mother was a leading authority on intestinal parasites, and whose schoolmates found out; whose father thought he'd be interested in Anglo-Saxon gerundives. Who was ignored by the au pairs till he was a teenager, and old enough to sleep with them. Or so he claims. Poor son, whose father never quashed the evil mother, was content with his own failure, and died early of his diabetes. Whose mother became a doting grandmother purely (thinks Donald) to rub his nose in it.

'Go on, then, dear,' says Meg contentedly, and lets him go with never another glance.

She says she's sorry she didn't come this morning, but she'd have thought Donald could manage to look after me for a few hours.

'I can see he hasn't. He's hopeless,' she says disapprovingly. 'Truly, Karin, it's not my fault. I did my best with him. The trouble was, he never liked me. He wouldn't drink my milk, you know. And the way he used to shout at me if I touched anything in his room! He's not so tidy in this house, is he? Anyway, he was most displeased with me that I didn't come over right away, but I couldn't let the other people down, could I? Oh, by the way, darling, this came for you. Donald said you were too ill for it, but I brought it up just the same.'

The letter has the details of the correspondence course about herbalism. Donald was right and – who knows – maybe his motivation for withholding it was better than I think.

'He's moving into the attic so as not to disturb you, he says. I'll make sure he doesn't come in for his things when you're asleep. It's a good job you've got so many rooms.'

9

My husband – what's his name, Erich? – has become utterly impossible. There's no rest from him, now he's home all the time.

He says his false teeth don't fit. He says he'll never work again. He says I shouldn't have found the lawyer to get him out of prison. He says I'm not feeding him properly, but it's the best I can do with the money – and he won't let me send the maid away. At least we have the rent from the flats he bought – we couldn't have afforded that if we'd had more children. How can I ask him to be cheerful? He spends all day in the living room, listening to the radio, news bulletin after news bulletin. I have to hear the speeches, crackling and rasping, loud, challenging, demanding, always demanding faith, hope, love.

Tramp, tramp, tramp, the boots are marching, all the way up to our door. The whole world believes in Hitler, except for a disreputable unconvincing straggle – Monika, Ursula, Tante Marlene, ourselves. No-one else to talk to, no-one else to talk to us.

And once a week Erich must take his hat and his stick and his coat (unless it's warm) and has to report to the police. He coughs sometimes: his chest was weakened in the cold cell. (The one he says I should have left him inside.)

Once a week I sit watching the door, and all the while he's not opening it, it seems impossible he might ever return. The clock ticks and strikes. They keep him waiting in there; who is he to expect prompt attention?

He comes home and warns me not to expect anything good of the future; there will be war, he says. He doesn't need to tell me, for how else will all this violence find an outlet?

I can't reach him. We're too far apart from each other. It feels lonelier than when he was locked up.

Always I shall see his face in the light of the flames at the Opernplatz, looking now at the university that threw him out, now at the students in brown shirts and red armbands who are hurling books onto the flames. One of those books is Erich's. Glowing sparks swarm above the fire and the wind blows the smoke this way and that; it gets in Erich's throat and he coughs, coughs, coughs. Faces are briefly, sharply lit. Supposing someone recognises us? And Erich puts his mouth to my ear and whispers bitterly, 'I'm not the only one who's come to watch himself go on the fire. There's Erich Kästner. Don't look now, though.'

And he wants me, when I feel as if I was stretched on the rack.

Please Erich, I promised to obey you, but don't touch me, leave me alone –

The rubber slips over the erect penis. I submit. Holy Mary, Mother of God, unsullied, eternal reproach to those of us who must –

This too I withheld from the priest. For marriage was ordained for the procreation of children.

'Erich, couldn't we have another baby?'

'Are you mad? Now? In these times? Do you want to bear cannon-fodder for Hitler's armies?'

I stand looking in the mirror at my own green eyes. My face

is strained till every feature seems a stranger to every other. And on Wednesdays Erich must put on his hat and his coat (unless it's warm) and report to the police. They used to say I was beautiful. It's a lie. I'm ugly, dull-faced, repulsive. And the neighbours all know where he's going and why. The neighbours know the truth about us. I have nothing to say to the accusers, they're inside me. They've convinced me. There is only one way to put a stop to this pain, this senselessness, this hatefulness.

I'm awake, shaken, Karin again, not Helene, who took an overdose of something – Veronal? I don't know. They pumped out her stomach and took her to the asylum. Anna probably saw them carry her away.

Helene delivered herself up to an adversary beyond controls, who has killed, mutilated and tormented throughout the ages, and has been rewarded by the gratitude and worship of its victims: the medical Moloch. I should know.

Didn't they lay me on my back to give birth to Elisabeth – for their convenience – making an exhausted woman push a baby uphill, against gravity, leaving me with a ragged hole between my legs? Could I forget those three months of increasing agony, or the refusal to admit it was their fault – or the consultant's remark after he did the repair: 'You're just the wrong shape to have a baby. Elective Caesarian next time, I think.' Only I fought. I was angry, I had my wits about me, I could demand a second opinion.

I wasn't carried off to an asylum, which means a place of safety, but not for the inmates. It's the people outside who need to feel safe. The broken and tormented, such as Helene, are an accusation best tidied out of the way. I wonder what platitudes they used? 'She's in the right place. They'll know what to do for her. There was nothing any of us can do'? How much of this did Anna listen to, and did she rebel, did she lie awake at night crying for her mother?

God knows it's bad enough when you have got your wits about you, you feel less than nothing in the huge maw of the hospital. If your soul has collapsed in tatters you haven't the shred of a right to speak for yourself, and no-one will speak for you.

She said once, 'There was a bed like a cage. I couldn't get out of it. They wouldn't listen to me. They put needles into me, then I lost time. I'll never get those days back again. Nobody came to see me. It was very lonely.' Maybe that wasn't true, maybe she didn't notice her visitors. In any case, she couldn't differentiate between any of her periods in hospital, when they'd filled her up with so many mind-bending drugs.

I believe her illness was her resistance, every time. But they slugged her into submission, and she had to come out and behave as they wanted.

Donald says, 'You'll have your work cut out to deal with the mess she's making in the kitchen.'

'But you'll give me a hand, won't you, Donald?' I say.

'Don't nag me,' says Donald. 'It's bad enough with Sally scratching away on that violin you insisted on buying her – she'd never make that racket if she had any talent –'

Interjection, by me, 'She's only just begun –'

Donald, as if I hadn't spoken '– and my mother drawing endless diagrams of the lifecycle of the tapeworm for Elisabeth. Why are women so disgusting? And if you insist on staying at home instead of looking for work –'

Interjection, by me, 'I'm going to send for the correspondence course in herbal medicine, Donald –'

Donald, as if I hadn't spoken, '– I wish you'd do the job properly. Look at that cobweb up in the corner.'

The sun is shining at just the right angle to catch the translucent silk of the cobweb in the corner, and to release a skein of delicate colour along its strands. Then one of the first flies of the season buzzes in through the window and straight into the web, shaking it violently. The spider hurries up, recoils from the trapped struggling fly, and retires to wait and watch. I can see its eyes gleaming. The fly is exhausting itself and getting ever more firmly entangled in the silky web, from which the light has fled.

I ought to think about Ursula Gruber, who lived in the house opposite Helene's, and was her friend. Who came to visit Helene when she came home from hospital and even brought her flowers as if she'd had a respectable illness. Helene first met Ursula when she took baby Anna to have her photograph taken. I have it now, Anna frowning at the camera as she lies naked on the studio's bearskin rug, and Ursula's name is scrawled in gold across the corner of the cardboard mount, though no-one would be able to book a sitting now.

Inside the apartment hung Ursula's work, the boys and girls in sailor suits, the official men with their uniforms and decorations, and the young women in their best clothes, but only a plate by the door outside, because it was a select neighbourhood. Ursula lived here with her husband till he was knocked down by a tram and killed. Ursula lost the baby she was carrying, and set about earning her own living. Her assistant, Hedwig, shared the apartment with her.

Omi said, 'Ursula was a good, kindhearted woman, and very devout.'

Monika said, 'I think she was a lesbian. There was something about her relationship with Hedwig, but she had to keep it discreet, of course, because in the Third Reich –'

At least Ursula was Aryan as far back as her grandparents, as she was obliged to certify. Having to prove his own and his wife's Aryan blood gave Erich something to do. People were encouraged to investigate as far back as they liked, and though Erich detested the reason, he enjoyed the practice. He was pleased to substantiate the family story that the Schäfers originated from the Austrian Tyrol, and had been exiled in the seventeenth century for their Protestantism. Ursula said she was far too busy to mess about with parish records any longer than she needed.

Ursula took Helene to church, giving her an arm to lean on all the way through the threatening busy streets, so helping her gently back into normal life (but the maid still did all the shopping), thus, I once heard my grandfather say in a temper to Anna, initiating his wife into the religious mania that was to do all the mischief.

The church was kind to her now: the Lord loves a broken and contrite spirit. The phrases jump so readily into my mind. I don't suppose I'll ever get rid of them. Even Anna left instructions for a proper Catholic funeral at the end. Why should I sneer? When Helene had given people even more cause to look askance at her, when Erich's manner showed she'd disgraced him, here was one place where she had to be nothing but what she was, and that was acceptable. (Was that why Peter went back to Catholicism, after his breakdown?) Though some churches displayed the swastika, Ursula's priest, to whom she took Helene, wouldn't hear of any such sacrilege. His solution was to say nothing about politics, but preach the Gospel, hoping some of his audience would draw their own conclusions. For Helene, it was enough to hear that Gospel, to cry and pray and rest in that other kingdom that had outlasted so much earthly power. She needed to speak to no-one except the priest who confessed her, and he was hidden by a screen. Forever afterwards she was to be content in that numinous world, like a child in her mother's lap.

While outside people were being kicked and throttled into custody, tortured till they signed everything, losing their civil rights and having their businesses daubed with obscenities. It was too late for Helene and Erich to be anything but paralysed.

10

Donald's drunk. His eyesockets are lined with red and his dark eyes are disreputable and trampish. He walks into the room, up to my bed, and comes to an unsteady halt, looking down at me.

'Donald,' I say.

He says, 'If you only knew what I'm going through.'

'What are you going through, Donald?' I'm scared.

'I can't tell you,' he says angrily. 'Shit, what I want is support, not interrogation.'

Meg is standing in the doorway, white-faced. I know that expression. She stood there like that listening to Donald and Anna last Boxing Day.

Donald says, 'We agreed, before we had the children, how things were going to be, and what you'd do when they went to school. It was a bloody good plan.'

'I've changed.'

'I know you now. Just remember that. You're impossible to satisfy, that's what it is. You'd wear a man out. You'd swallow him, and you'd still be hungry. You want this, you want that. God Almighty.'

I feel so tired. I wish he'd go away.

'You're a whirlpool,' says Donald. And out he goes, ignoring Meg, who comes in to sit down heavily on the bed beside me.

'Karin,' she says, 'do you think he's having a breakdown?' Her hair is falling down, an unwinding silver rope. 'Karin,' her voice is shaking, she's sobbing, 'do you think it is my fault?'

If he heard that, he must be laughing.

'I'm going down,' she says, blowing her nose. 'The state he's in, I don't trust him with the children.'

'Yes, please, Meg.'

Isn't he the whirlpool? How do I know what's going on in his head? He says he knows me; he doesn't. He knows what he wants to make of me. And I don't know him. All these years we've laughed together, been naked together, made children together, planned, chatted – acting a farce.

And if he really was having a breakdown? If Meg were to find him as we found Peter, wrists gaping, blood puddling the bathroom floor? (You screwed him up, the poor lad.) I haven't the strength to control my thoughts or be sensible or pull myself together; am I disintegrating too? Is the earth spinning above my head, as it did above Peter's when he brought his fighter jet out of the clouds? (I ought to have trusted the instruments, it's very dangerous to go by your own sensations. But there was so much turbulence, I could hardly see anything. The plane was jumping all over the place. I wasn't making sense.)

If he were to do as Peter did, wouldn't I blame myself? (I managed to pull the plane out of the dive – I got down all right, but next time I was up in cloud I thought the whole thing was starting off again. I don't know why I can't get over it. I told them I couldn't fly, and they sent me home to get over it, but I won't. I know I'll never fly again.) I was scared of him, wreck though he was. There wasn't a key to my door, so I pushed my dressing table against it instead. (I'll come to your room, he'd written. Anna won't have to know anything about it.) I only had to do that for two nights. Then Dad was there, having a shouting match with Anna after he came back from the hospital. Peter will never lose the scars of his colleagues' antagonism and contempt. Lack of moral fibre, they called it. I felt such a fool, when Anna came to my door and found it barricaded. Worse, guilty. You'd think I'd threatened him. She couldn't stand it, that was why. Her mother was dead, and now this. At least Dan, her lover, was very good to her.

Oh, God, he's back again, and he really seems to be paralytic now, but with that friendly expression on his face, he doesn't seem to be suffering.

He's seen some book about marital sex that's proved to him how it's damaged women to feel they ever need orgasm, how much better it is for them to concentrate on being a perfect, well-dressed housewife and hostess, how they ought to find their pleasure in fostering their husband's. He's rambling about Louis XV's mistress, who set out to feel nothing. Have an orgasm, don't have an orgasm, it's what's behind the messages that counts.

He's sitting down on the bed beside me, breathing whisky

into my face. He's stripping me verbally – he knows this much about me, that I have lumpy scar tissue between my legs, stretch marks on my breasts and belly, small, he admits, but damning, that the skin is loosening and creasing round my eyes, and whereas age lends distinction to a man and makes him more attractive –

He has got another woman. I wish he'd run off with her.

– Donald says, with all these handicaps, if I want to keep him, I'll have to work at it instead of endlessly demanding things for myself.

'Donald, I'll talk to you when you're sober.'

But his face is changing, a shudder running across it, he has to get up and hurry – as best he can – to the bathroom. He's being loudly, revoltingly sick. Well, at least he made the loo.

Here is Meg.

'Where is he?'

'In the bathroom.'

She goes to him. She's telling him to get up – I wonder what he's doing? – to go and sleep it off.

'Karin, I'm dreadfully sorry, but I can't move him, he's really made a thorough job of this – I'm going to have to ask you for help.'

This is wonderful. One day I can't get up without keeling over, the next I've got to heave my drunken husband about. At least he hasn't attacked me – not physically. I'm still privileged.

He's got such a silly satisfied grin on his face, this must feel really good to him, and I'm prickling and sweating as we lug him along the corridor, he's co-operating just enough to make it possible, he's even making an effort when we get to the attic stairs. I hope he has a filthy hangover in the morning. There are little black flecks dancing in front of my eyes. And Meg with her back trouble. Watch him flop on the bed. Donald Pasha.

'Go and lie down now, love,' says Meg. 'Be careful on the stairs.'

Thank God for the banister, and that the attic stairs aren't as narrow as some.

I need to sleep. The phone. It's never been unplugged. So I pick it up (fool).

'Karin Birkett.'

'Hi, Karin, this is Sam Larsen. I'm calling from Chicago. Is Donald there?'

Now what do I say to his American co-director? What the hell.

'Yes, he is.'

'Can I speak to him?' He's surprised I haven't scampered off already - it's my job, after all, to run round after my husband.

'I wouldn't. He's so drunk I don't think you'd get much sense out of him.'

Horrified pause. I want to cackle, I have the malice but not the courage. One day -

'Oh,' says Sam. 'I see.' (He sounds as if I'd threatened to detonate a bomb in his office.) 'I'll call him tomorrow. Thank you. Goodbye!'

Pity he didn't leave a message. I wouldn't have written it down.

I stagger into the bathroom and inspect the wrinkles around my eyes and the dark hollows under them. I'm hanging on with this marriage for the sake of the children, but I don't have to. I have my own money, I could let the spare room and the attic to lodgers.

I'm going to write to Bernt, and ask him what he knows about Helene that I might not know. Right now. I've got some paper and envelopes in the dressing table.

I start the letter in German - dare I use the curious hybrid mixture of English and German that was ours? No. German, all the way through.

Dear Bernt, I suppose you will be surprised to hear from me. (Dear Bernt, this may be a shock to you, but I'm getting married.) *The thing is that I have been going through a difficult time since my mother died.* (Asking for sympathy – pfui.) *I am so sorry I never answered your kind letter,* (Donald is finishing a thesis in microbiology and intends to start a consultancy with some other Oxford scientists. We are going to marry as soon as I have done my Schools, and instead of the Diplomatic Service I am going to work for a D.Phil. It will be a struggle at first, but I think I am going to enjoy my life. What did I think I was writing? A job application for Donald? I love him and feel safe with him. Ha, ha.) *but you must realise that Anna's was a death terrible shock. I had to go to identify her body, which was hideously burned. Then there was the inquest, and the publicity, and journalists – because of the circumstances – besieging me at home and asking intrusive questions, and I shall be glad if I never see another journalist again in all my life. I suppose you heard the rumours that it might have been suicide. Anna was a very private person and she would have wanted to die alone, not taking all those people with her. That may sound odd, but it is the truth.*

I can feel his body at rest against mine, stockier than Donald's, and hairier, but defenceless. I don't know how to go on. I might find myself writing the words of the other letter, about having wanted the wrong things, understanding at last that I wanted marriage, a house with a garden where I could watch things grow, and children. Well, I do value the garden, and I have the children. Out of all this snarl came Elisabeth and Sally. And there is Meg. If I'd gone into the diplomatic service, I'd have had to accommodate as I've been doing for the last fourteen years, and I might have woken up equally nauseated, without my daughters. Would I ever have made a diplomat? It would have staggered my teachers.

It has become very important to me to find out as much as I can about Omi's life, in which way I am also finding out about Anna's. I don't quite understand why, but the reason I am writing to you is that I wonder if you know anything I don't. I'm asking a lot – I'm sure you're busy – but if you could scribble down what you remember about her (scribble, on a word processor?) *and post it to me, you'd be doing me a great favour. I hope all is well with you and your work, and with*

Ulrike. (Does she live with him, I wonder?) *Greetings to her, and to you, from Karin.*

That's done.

11

Helene said, 'There'd always been talk of air-raids, and gas, and there was an Air-Raid Protection League as early as 1935.' That was the year Uncle Robert joined the RAF and began to train as a pilot, in a tin-can aircraft quite different from the ergonomic wonders they put Peter in.

'I remember one day we were waiting to cross the road and a horsedrawn float came along, with a bomb on it – I don't know if it was a real one. There were people in gasmasks sitting round the bomb, as if they were its courtiers, Karin. They belonged to this Air-Raid Protection League, and so did the men who were handing out leaflets, what was it? Yes. GET YOUR GASMASK NOW.

'We were shopping – I was making a party dress for Anna – we'd bought some mull-muslin with blue rosebuds. There was an old woman beside us, complaining because she couldn't cross the road; she said she had her work to get on with, and things were bad enough the way it was normally with the traffic, and that when she was a nipper, you could get across the road, your nerves weren't strained to breaking every five minutes. Then she said of course the Führer had done wonderful things, he'd made it more like the Kaiser's day than she'd have believed possible, and that was why she wasn't getting a gasmask yet. She believed the Führer when he said there wasn't going to be a war.

'But Anna had taken one of the leaflets, and she read it through. She said, "Imagine, Mutti, everything just the same as usual, and they drop gas on us, and we all die. But the streets would be just the same, wouldn't they, and everything would be in the shops." She made me shiver.'

Omi sighed, and went inside herself. I would have left her, but she said, 'And of course, most people did feel calm and comfortable. We were getting the Olympic Games in Berlin the next year. There was no litter on the streets, or dead bodies, the way there often had been under the Republic.' Helene laughed bitterly, as I'd never heard her before. 'You see, people weren't allowed to drop litter on the street, and the corpses were kept tidily out of sight. They'd opened the first stretch of autobahn, and everybody had a radio.'

'Well, naturally,' said Monika. 'We had to have a radio. How else would they have got their propaganda across?'

A story becomes your own, and it changes. I don't know how much of this happened as I see it in my mind, formed as it is on a framework of anecdote, fleshed out by other people's accounts, discoloured by memory and distorted by subsequent events and my own prejudice. I am trying to be honest. Who can do more?

Helene said that one day she begged Erich to get them out of Germany. She asked him to get a job in Switzerland or even America. She begged him, even though she was frightened. If they went to Switzerland, she'd understand the language, but she'd forgotten the English she'd learned, and she knew she'd be lost in America.

'I only suggested it because the days were so long and the hours so dreary,' she said, 'and yet I was afraid. I couldn't enjoy Anna, I didn't know what was going to become of her. And sometimes the fear grew so sharp I thought it'd choke me. I never thought of England. It's strange that I never thought I'd end up living in England.' She smiled painfully. It was then it occurred to me how difficult it must have been for her to be uprooted to an alien country full of incomprehensible conversations. How could I have been so insensitive? She was Omi, that was why, she had always been there, patiently waiting for someone to talk to her in German.

I put my arm round her, but she sat straight, brittle against my embrace; she had to finish the story whose bitterness couldn't be contained any longer.

'Erich only said, "You shouldn't run to church so much. Do you think they don't know about it?" I was horrified – I stared at him – then I saw he was quite white. I hadn't noticed it happening. I saw he might easily try to take his own life. He had lost so much. I said, "Erich, I have to pray. It's all I can do." He said, "You can pray at home, can't you?" I said that was what they wanted, that everyone would stop going to church, would follow this new state religion and Hitler. I said I couldn't stop going anyway, not even to save my life. I could breathe in church. And the child had to have Communion, and they were closing all the Catholic schools. I asked him if he wanted her to burn in hell?'

Her voice had become panicky and breathless as it must have been when she told him all this. And he was frightened of her instability, so he propitiated her, and said he didn't want to stop her going. She knew.

'He treated me differently since I'd been ill, like a child, except that he wasn't frightened of the child. I asked again why we didn't leave. Because Monika was marrying, and going to live in Bad Godesberg. Klaus-Peter was Tante Marlene's husband's cousin – he had no Jewish blood, and of course by then it was against the law for Aryans and Jews to marry. It was worse than that: Jews were state subjects without rights, but who had rights anyway, at that time? Certainly not your grandfather. Klaus-Peter was a good man, he was going to adopt Josef. I knew Monika would be happy with him. I said there was nothing to keep us in Berlin. But he said, "It's no use. They wouldn't have us." I said, why not? They knew his work, he had friends over there, he spoke good English, we could sell the apartments to get the money –'

Again, her voice was speeding up, her breath was short. It was as if she was racing to tell me the story before her strength gave out. 'He said, "It's you. They wouldn't take you because of your illness." '

Was he trying to torment her? He'd done his best not to say it, but once it was out, he went on, 'You'd better not have another breakdown, or I can't guarantee your life.'

She said, 'I knew what he meant. We heard rumours. I was going about again, now. I was talking to people. Someone told me about the mentally sick people they took away from hospitals in coaches with blacked-out windows, and then their relatives got a telegram saying they had died unexpectedly of pneumonia. They might put another needle in me, and I'd lose time for ever. I said, "It wouldn't matter so much, if it weren't for the child –" '

She rubbed her forehead. I knew she had a headache.

'He said, "Don't say that! What would I do without you?" He was crying, Karin.'

And so was she by now, talking and crying in my arms.

'Then Herr Schenk came to the door, the Blockwart – he was collecting for the Winter Aid, and we knew he'd report how much we put in. Your grandfather hated to give the money – he knew it was going for armaments. And that was another thing. He was certain a war was coming, and he didn't want to fight against his own country.'

I asked, 'Was it really dangerous, just going to church?'

She said, 'That depended on the priest, or the pastor.'

Monika said, 'I used to bring them treats, but your grandfather didn't like it. They had to be very careful about money, because Erich was determined to keep the maid, Klara. And yet, at that time, she was patronising them, and doing just as she liked. She kept getting extra money out of them, too. There was a Jewish family downstairs, the Blumenthals, they had an old Aryan maid, she'd been with them forever. Klara prattled about how foolish the other maid was not to have asked for a rise at least, when it was such a dubious post, and by the way, did Frau Doktor know Frau Schenk had just got the Mother Cross for her fifth baby – Herr Schenk was the concierge, he lived on the top floor with his family – and what a pity she didn't have any help with all those children – later on, the Party sent her a succession of young girls. Then Klara span them some yarn about another family that wanted her, and they gave her a rise. The jibes about the children were what really hurt Helene. Oh, and then she moved the chiffonnier over to the other side of the room – it looked peculiar there, but she insisted it made cleaning easier. Helene let it happen.'

Helene said, 'Your grandfather said we could hold our heads up if we kept the maid.'

Then there was 1936. The year of the Olympiad. The year they took down the abusive placards that sent Jews away from anything Aryans were able to enjoy. (Probably they'd internalised the messages by then.) The year everyone, at home and abroad, thought Hitler was maturing, and that things would get better. When the Blumenthals cancelled their emigration to America, Klara said, 'Why shouldn't they stay? The father has the Iron Cross, he fought for the Fatherland just like my own poor husband in France, God rest him.' I can see Berlin swamped with a complacency as clouded as the famous white beer, happy that the world was coming to visit after years of social ostracism.

The police told Erich he had served his probation, and didn't need to call on them any more. Helene said he changed overnight. He took up a few contacts and found himself a management position in industry – was it steel? Monika said, 'And my sister told the maid to move the chiffonier back against the other wall, which was where she wanted it. Klara obeyed.'

Monika had married in early December 1935 – I have the photo. There is Klaus-Peter with his arm round Monika, half a head shorter than her and very pleased with himself. I think he hoped she wasn't too old, at thirty-six, to give him a child. He may also have recognised what a brilliant business partner she was going to make him. She revolutionised the firm. Besides, she was good company, handsome and sexy – I can see that in the picture, and you could see it even in her old age. Bernt's way of looking at you and speaking to you was like hers. And here is Marlene, old and light and lively-looking, and here is my great-uncle Karl, who may still be alive in East Germany for all I know. Monika had asked her father to the wedding; he didn't even answer. But Karl came, bringing his new wife – she looks very provincial here, and unsure of herself. Helene in particular is very elegant, though there's no ornament on her dark clothes. Erich is straight and proud. Anna is dressed in the mull-muslin with blue rosebuds, but Josef is a Hitler Youth, brown and leather-strapped. He stayed with my grandparents while Monika and Klaus-Peter were on honeymoon. Then they put him on a west-bound train and watched his waving arm disappear – Helene was terrified to see him lean out of the window, in spite of all her warnings, but he reached Bonn with head and neck intact.

Helene wrote to her father every month, asking for forgiveness. It did no good.

'Erich wasn't directly involved in munitions at that stage,' said Monika, 'but his firm was expanding its manufacture of certain components, and that was partly why they took him on. He was good at his job, and they promoted him. He was hard-working and intelligent, a good administrator and a good manager. He had authority with the workforce, because he was scrupulously just, and so he earned respect.'

At home, however, he became bumptious – that's the only way I can interpret what I was told.

'Opa was very strict, and sometimes he could seem too hard, especially when he said Anna's paintings and drawings were rubbish, and threw them in the stove.'

'I can hear him, "What's this meant to be? Why are you wasting your time? What sort of school report are you going to bring home if you waste your time with this sort of rubbish? What else has she got in her room?" I can see Anna, sullen and silent, fiddling with her two long plaits while her secret life was fetched out for her father's condemnation. She had to watch as he took the drawings and paintings up one by one in his disgusted hands, abused each one, then scrumpled the lot up and stuffed them into the stove. Paper burns fast.'

'He said it was bent, perverted – he used horrible words. He said, "What is the girl, what has she got in her head?" But you see, what she was drawing was the sort of thing the Party had called decadent. People weren't allowed to exhibit such work. And of course, he was concerned for the child.'

Of course.

'She had to do her homework under my eye, after that. But I didn't look too carefully where the paper and pencils went, and she hid her work under the mattress.'

Then he started on her Church. 'He was a Lutheran, he didn't understand. They were persecuting monks and nuns for things they couldn't have done –' She shuddered, and her face closed up. Did he say there was no smoke without fire, that he'd always wondered what they were up to, shut up together in those monasteries? She said, 'My own priest was taken away, when he found he had to preach against the government. Erich said we must take the rough with the smooth, and wasn't I pleased that the Rhineland was German again?'

She was thirty-five now, and her face wasn't quite young any more. Her eyes, large and beautiful, were haunted by a melancholy that was only to intensify. She wore white, grey, dark colours, a lot of black – but with her colouring they must have looked stunning. She parted her hair in the centre and drew it loosely back to a knot at the nape of her neck.

She looks at me out of the photograph. She doesn't recognise me; that woman didn't know me yet. She knew only her thin, frowning, secretive daughter.

I can hear the older Helene's voice: 'I began to feel bad again, I couldn't understand why, when everything was supposed to be getting better. I felt like two people, Karin, one was the shell, carrying on as normal, but inside I was huddling up for fear. The worst thing was when we had to entertain and go out, and I thought I could sense other people's feelings, underneath all their laughter and confidence and talk I thought they were as frightened as I was. We were all pretending. And since your grandfather had got his good job, the regime had come to live with us at home. I told the doctor I was getting breathless, and he gave me something to inhale. And he gave me something to make me sleep. It made me feel ill in the mornings, but I took it. How could I refuse? I didn't want them to come for me again, I had the child.' And then she said: 'The only thing that saved me was the Church.'

12

With my arms round Meg, I can smell her old hair and skin, feel how much more fragile she is than I, even though I've been ill. I do love her.

'Drive carefully, Meg, won't you?' I couldn't bear it if I lost her. I can't let go of her, I know she has her own life to lead, but I wish she could stay another week. Her hand on my shoulder becomes Anna's hand, Helene's hand; once she's dead I'll have nothing to do but wait for my own old age.

Doubtfully, she asks Donald to take care of me. She's cooked meals for the next week and put them in the freezer. Donald says he'll make sure I don't overdo it. Meg says it needs more than words. Donald says yes, of course. He sounds so nice, so normally solicitous of me. Meg stares at him.

His phone call from the States last night has made a different man of him.

Meg gets into her car and drives out onto the road, missing the gatepost by a centimetre or less. (When you've driven with her, you find it hard to believe she's never had a single accident: you'd think the car had been left to its own judgement.)

Donald says he's taking the day off so he can clean the house and deal with the kitchen and fetch the children from school. He says he's sorry for everything he said and did. Can we forget about it and start again?

We ought to be fading into the sunset to the sound of an ahhing choir, in each other's arms, as he takes me now, white cherry blossom tossing above our heads, birds singing –

'I've no right to dictate what you do with your life. It's up to you. If you want to do this herbalism course, who am I to object, darling?'

He kisses me again, getting more passionate, and I can feel myself responding, so I'm pleased to go upstairs with him, and perhaps a good fuck can make things better.

He's treating me so very kindly, with so much consideration, he's doing everything he can think of to turn me on; and from the moment he enters me I feel nothing. Absolutely nothing. He's heavy, and I can't breathe with his mouth on mine. It would be better for the children if we stayed together. I'll see what happens.

Come on, Donald, get it over with. I'm tired.

Anna is to have a retrospective exhibition at the Tate, no less. They want me to be interviewed for the television programme – forget it. Anyway, Anna wouldn't have wanted anything personal – let them look at her work and find her there. Maybe Dan will talk to them, but he won't let anything much out, even under interrogation.

I'll have to go to the private view, though. I wonder if Peter will come? There'll be critics and theatre people as well as other artists – Dan, of course – he probably lobbied for it in the first place. There'll be journalists – I can feel hairs go up on the back of my neck – looking for signs of neurosis and self-destructiveness in her work, so they can write a clever article belittling her, determined to be dismissive, some of them, because they know a woman couldn't be an artist of the first rank. They want to borrow the paintings. But do I show them the fabric collage she did here, on the kitchen table and all over the floor, when the children asked her why she was cutting such tiny pieces? It was a step into a new world. If only she'd looked in her rearview mirror.

Do I? I couldn't keep it from Donald. He'll have to come to the private view. And we're being nice to each other at the moment, and it's satisfactory, though not satisfying. If our marriage is to be stuck and riveted together for the children's sake, surely I'd better leave the collage rolled up under the spare room wardrobe?

She left it behind by accident. She meant to take it with her. I know how she felt about her work.

I've got a headache.

'You really want to know what it was like?' Anna turned on me one day, savagely. 'I'll tell you what it was like. One night I came into the living room and my father was reading my mother a maths textbook he'd found in the tram – a boys' book. They didn't notice me. All the examples were to do with ideology – geometry in terms of the Aryan profile and the dimensions of the skull, arithmetic in terms of how many children you needed to keep the population expanding. I listened, because my own books had none of that, though we had measured each others' skulls once, in class. And suddenly my father's face lost the sarcastic expression, and he stopped reading. My mother asked, "What is it?" and he said, "Nothing. There's nothing more to read." But she didn't believe him, she reached out and took the book from him, and read the next question aloud, "If an estate of workers' flats costs so much, and a lunatic asylum costs so much, how many workers' flats could be built for the cost of one asylum?" Then she said, "Yes, I see." She looked as if all the life had drained out of her face, and yet it was my father who was shaking and he seized the book from her – quite roughly – and pushed it into the stove.'

'Then they saw me. They didn't know how long I'd been watching them, and I could see from their faces they didn't know what to say. Because they never told me anything, do you hear? Nobody told me what was going on, or explained the things they couldn't hide from me. Vati's gone away for a while, he'll soon be back. Mutti's gone away for a while, she's going to be all right. Don't be afraid. Don't cry. Don't ask questions. I never told them about the girl who taunted me at school, who said my mother was going to be killed, and I wouldn't be allowed to marry or have children because of her illness. It wasn't just that she had to be protected. I felt as if I'd imagined all these things, as if they'd never happened, even when they took Vati, that had been a bad dream. And you ask me didn't I know what was happening to the Jews?'

I wonder what they said to her about the night of the ninth of November, 1938? I don't know.

Helene told me that she and Erich were at a concert of sacred music – she didn't say what, though it wouldn't have been Israel in Egypt or Judas Maccabeus. Both might have been appropriate. They took a taxi home, she said – that is, they started in a taxi.

'The driver stopped. He said he was worried about what the broken glass might do to his tyres. He said he was sorry, and we'd better take the tram. He wanted to get home, and see what was going on there. He said it was shameful. He thought the Führer had put a stop to this sort of thing. Shameless hooligans, he called them, who didn't deserve to be called Berliners. By the end of the tram ride we had seen plenty of the sort of things that were happening.' I think they passed the burning synagogue in the Fasanenstrasse, among other sights.

They understood this was an action against Jews.

Helene said, 'I thought of the Blumenthals. The little one wasn't well, she had a shadow on her lung. Erich said, "They won't set the house on fire, it's only the synagogue I've seen on fire." '

Maybe fear and whispering are habit-forming, and in any case there were other people on the tram. She said she was frightened the squads might come for them, too, but she didn't dare ask him if he felt the same.

She said, 'It seemed unreal, looking at it from the tram, like the wars you see on the television now, but I knew when the ride ended we'd have to go out into it.

'The tram took us round a corner. There was a man being dragged away from a group of brutes who were thrashing an older man – they had him on the ground.' She caught a sobbing breath of empathy.

'Then we were pulled away, round another corner, and in these streets there was nothing happening, the drawn curtains made it look like a peaceful night. Only you could see the glow of the burning synagogue in the sky above the houses. In the next street there was a Jewish-owned antique shop – I knew it, I used to like looking at the things on display there – we were getting very near home. There was no glass left in the windows, it was all on the pavement in front of the building, mixed up with pieces of the Bohemian crystal and Dresden and Sèvres porcelain, and they were burning the beautiful furniture on the pavement. An old woman behind me said, "Disgusting. It shouldn't be allowed, and there's a policeman standing there. What have things come to, such a rabble –" and Opa nudged me and said, "Get up. It's our stop." The tram arrived exactly on time. He said, "Everything's quiet here." '

They walked the three hundred yards and arrived at the house door at the same moment as a truckload of honest citizens turned the corner.

She said, 'Opa told me to go upstairs, but I wouldn't.' She could be immovably stubborn, when she knew she was right. She told me, 'I knew I had to warn the Blumenthals. Opa thought there wouldn't be time, but they lived on the ground floor, so I pushed the bell. Herr Blumenthal came to the door; I could see his wife and daughters behind him, and they were a little afraid, not much. I wasn't afraid. Not at all.' She paused to wonder at herself.

'I said they must come upstairs and not ask any questions, because there wasn't time. Opa whispered that the people would come looking for them in our flat. I took no notice. And yet Anna was asleep up there. The Blumenthals understood. That was a good thing.' It had happened to their grandparents and great-grandparents and their grandparents. The pogrom. Only in this generation Herr Blumenthal felt German enough to reach for his Iron Cross where it hung on the wall behind him.

'He said they wouldn't hurt a distinguished veteran. He told his wife and the girls to go up with us. We didn't argue. There wasn't time. We got into our own living room as the first stone came through the Blumenthals' window.'

Well-off people pay for apartments with good thick walls: all they could hear was the smashing and falling of glass. Did Vati Blumenthal manage to say anything of what he'd rehearsed?

She said, 'We didn't switch the light on, we crept to the window, and there was Herr Blumenthal, he still had the Iron Cross in his hand, and they were dragging him out to beat him up on the pavement. Frau Blumenthal – she had one hand over her mouth as if she could hold it inside her, the agony – she tried to push the girls away, so they wouldn't see it, but the girls wouldn't go. Only Opa went and threw himself into a chair. He lay there with a hand over his face. I couldn't look away. One of them punched Herr Blumenthal to the ground, and the Iron Cross rolled away from his hand, and stamp, his hand lay splayed and still. They kicked his head, and he couldn't protect it. Then you could see nothing but boots, and I was crying, too: I'd seen it before. And the men stood back and laughed at his bloodied face. We knelt by the window. Nobody made a sound.

'They picked him up by his heels and his shoulders and slung him roughly into the back of their truck. There were other men there, but I couldn't make them out. If only he had come upstairs! Opa went to the cupboard where we kept the brandy. He said, "Sit down. All of you." Then he made us all drink. We needed it. We could hear them downstairs, throwing things out of the window and singing the Horst

Wessel song; we found clothes, gramophone records, pot plants, china, everything, the next day. And blood. There was dry blood on the street. Opa drank his brandy and ran his hands over his face, as if he was trying to reassure himself it hadn't been him this time.'

She said none of them could say anything about what had happened. It seemed so monstrous, they couldn't any of them take it in. Not even Frau Blumenthal and the girls. And Anna was asleep, they thought she slept through the whole of that unholy night.

She said, 'The next day all the women in the house, and Ursula and Hedwig, helped tidy and clean the Blumenthals' apartment, yes, even Frau Schenk with her Nazi Mother Cross, though she did ask Frau Blumenthal if she wasn't going to emigrate. But how could they go, when the father was supposed to be in the camp at Sachsenhausen? – though what he'd done nobody understood, or why the family had to pay a fine for what had been done to them. People realised, then, that Hitler didn't stand for law and order. But when you had to be so careful who you spoke to –'

The fabric collage really looks very good. I have to send it to the gallery, and let them make the decision. I can't suppress it; I can't silence her like that.

13

The phone. It's Gail, about Sally's violin. She wants to ring me now, she says, to tell me (without Sally listening) that Sally is amazingly good – I must have noticed the progress she's made. She says she's never taught anyone like her. Sally has gone further in four weeks than most children do in a year, and her musicality – and her touch – and the feeling – oh, yes, she knows I'm musical, but this is different.

I thank Gail for phoning, and say I'm pleased to hear Sally is doing so well. Fortunately, being a musician, Gail is more likely to be demanding than to encourage any illusions.

I'm nervous of a reply from Bernt. I shouldn't have written to him. If he doesn't answer, it'll mean he's given up forgiving me. That would be a good thing.

She said, 'The telephone rang. And I picked it up, thinking it was Ursula, or Marlene. It was Monika. I was pleased to hear her. She said, "Lenchen, our father's dead." He hadn't answered any of my letters. I asked her where she was, hoping she was speaking from Bad Godesberg, but she said she was in Silesia.'

He had sent for the unrepentant daughter, keeping Helene at bay. He hadn't even spoken of her. Was she angry with Monika for going where Helene wasn't wanted? Did she suppress the unchristian thought, and hate herself for it? When Monika said the stepmother wanted Helene there for the funeral, did she want to slam the receiver down, abuse Monika, say she'd stay away? If she did, she'd have felt it was the Devil's prompting.

'Anna came in from collecting scrap metal. I said, "Your grandfather's dead. I have to go to his funeral." I couldn't take Anna, she was too young. Opa had too much to do at work. I booked my ticket for the next day and told Opa when he came home. He was very tired. He sighed, and sat down,' (probably with the slippers Anna had brought him).

'He asked me to go to see his own father while I was there – put flowers on his grave, that is. I said, "We'll soon be running out of flowers." He sighed again. He said yes, that was how it was going. He said Hitler and Stalin were going to cut Poland up like a cake between them. And I had no elder brothers left. I wondered how many younger brothers I'd have by the time it was over. Even little Jörgen was old enough to fight. And my Michael. Maybe even Josef. I said, "Do I have to be grateful I have no sons?" He said, "Yes, you do. Now you must get some rest; you have all that way to go in the morning." '

Cruel, self-righteous, and yet concerned.

She felt no-one wanted the war, except Hitler and his friends, who knew war was the best way to hang onto their credibility.

They stood round the grave, all in black except for Jörgen in his Wehrmacht uniform (he was doing military service). Karl was thirty, heavily built, and already the father of a son, Michael had grown amazingly plump, and Gustav amazingly insignificant, in spite of his auburn hair just like Helene's. Hanna was mousey, looked like her mother and had been engaged for four years. Helene said she didn't dare weep. She said her father had refused her permission to repent, and he'd left her with her sins: nothing could be done for her now.

'The coffin was terribly heavy,' said Monika. 'The men were glad to let go of it. It was hot, and breathless. He had died of cancer, and my stepmother said it was a merciful release. She was quite exhausted; he'd been impossible, I saw that. It was as if the Devil had got into him at the end. Helene took it all to herself; she thought his illness, his bad behaviour, our stepmother's exhaustion, everything was her fault. Maybe she even thought the war was her fault.'

Monika's hand made a little despairing stamp on the arm of her chair.

'There was a warm, sticky wind blowing from the east,' she said, 'making the wreaths dusty. It coated you with sweat. God, those black clothes were hot!'

It was the fifteenth of August. In the evening Monika and Helene talked in the garden and saw stars falling out of the sky.

'We knew it'd start when the grain was in,' Monika said. 'I wasn't sure if England and France would fight for Poland, but Helene said they wouldn't stand by and watch for ever. I knew she was right. Most people hoped they would. They said, "leave him to it," as if they weren't involved. I had a cigar out there. I hadn't smoked one in the house, in case our stepmother was shocked. She'd had enough to put up with. Helene said, and she spoke too loudly, "Why is it happening? Who wants it? So many people are going to be killed, and all we can do is wait for it to happen!" I asked, "What can you do?" I still ask that. What could we have done? I didn't know anyone I could conspire with. I wasn't an aristocrat, or a Communist.

'We heard someone walking towards us in the darkness – there was a path of silence among the cricket calls. We stopped talking. It was Michael. He asked, "Is that you, Monika, smoking a cigar?" I gave him one; he lit it. We stood there smoking cigars, thinking about the end of the world. I can still see the stars darting down and disappearing behind the dark gable of the house. Michael said, "You should be careful what you say." We couldn't see the expression on his face, and we didn't know what he had become. The crickets were chirping the way they do any warm night, and we were in the garden where we played when we were children. The cigars smelt good. Helene said she didn't expect her own family to betray her. But that was bravado, when we were both so careful what we said in front of our children. They might have repeated something in all innocence. Oh, we kept them innocent; it was safer, in those days. Their minds had to be free for Hitler to poison.

'Michael said, "*Ach, Gott*, if it's going to come it might as well come at once and have done." He was bitter. He'd only just got engaged. And the wind was still blowing from Poland, and in the morning the petals were already quite brown on the memorial flowers.'

The phone rings. I pick it up. An American voice wants Donald.

'I'm sorry,' I say. 'He's not here at the moment. Can I take a message?'

'Is he in the States, Mrs Lowe?'

It can't be one of Donald's American colleagues: they all know what to call me.

'No,' I say. 'Who is that speaking?'

A minute hesitation, then, 'My name's John Watson. Will he be going to the States in the next four weeks?'

There's something here I don't like. Whoever I'm speaking to, I'm certain his name's not John Watson.

'If you want to contact him next time he goes to the States, you could ring his office and fix it up with him. I couldn't give you any details of his itineraries.' Then I add, 'I'll tell him you called.'

'Well,' reluctantly, 'in fact he doesn't know me.'

(No, it sounds like it. What is this about? I'm getting rattled.)

'Which firm are you from?'

'I work for myself.'

'If you'd like to leave a number he can ring you back at?'

Perceptible hesitation. He gives a number I'm sure is completely random. I write it down all the same.

Helene said, 'I told the maid that Doktor Schäfer didn't like us to deal on the black market. I said she mustn't get her cousin to slip her anything under the counter. She said she understood, but I had my suspicions. She thought I had my head in the clouds, too good for this world – apart from my illness, and she did her best to pretend that hadn't happened. I didn't ask too many questions, and I didn't try to match the ration books to what I found in the kitchen. Because I didn't care. I hated the war, and rationing was part of it. I didn't want to be patriotic and go without as Erich thought we should. I wanted to feed my family.'

This was the phony war, the joke war. The Blumenthals were still in their flat, and Elli was coughing more than ever. There wouldn't have been many places she was allowed to go looking for fresh air – Jewish children had to play in the cemeteries. But she and her mother and sister had been set to work, early till late at a munitions factory. Thousands of bacilli she must have sprayed over the bullets and cartridges. Who cared?

The winter came iron-hard, one of the winters people remember for years on end, the sort that dominate thoughts during peacetime and phony wars. Erich was coughing, but struggled to work every day: Helene worried that he might have TB too. He said nonsense, it was nothing.

Coughcoughcough. Wheeze. He recovered his breath and insisted, in a voice that fizzed with unsolved irritation in the throat, 'It'll be gone in a day or so.' I can hear him. I can see him going down the stairs, into the white world outside to run for his tram, Helene looking out, losing his dark figure among the scurrying flakes of snow.

He might never have heard of the worst address in Berlin, the Gestapo Centre in the Prinz-Albrechtstrasse. He was obsessed by the need to do his work properly – the firm now only made components for the war, and what, specifically, did they compose? Bombs. (What did you do in the war, Opa?)

Helene said, 'He never said he was doing it for the Führer, he never used that title at home. He might praise this or that of the regime's actions – less since the war started – he never praised Hitler, he was doing it for us. He said the war should never have begun, but now we must all join to avoid defeat. He thought only strength could bring an honourable peace.

'There wasn't enough food, because it was freezing and spoiling in the stores. Soon there wasn't enough coal and they begged us not to use the electricity: they said it was needed in industry. Opa coughed all winter, but he wouldn't let us fetch out the electric heater.'

Coughcoughcough. 'You'll thank me for it one day.' Cough. 'All those irresponsible parasites, certainly not.' Coughcoughcough.

She said, 'He even took the plug off the electric heater. But when Anna had a cough, too, what could I do? Klara taught me how to wire a plug, and we put the plug on as soon as he'd gone out, and stayed in the living room as much as we could, and before he came home one of us took it off again.' As she told me this a look of shy mischief came into her face – she hadn't ever taken in the propaganda, she'd enjoyed the deception, and so, I'd bet, did Klara.

'Anna's cough got better. Her school was shut because of the cold, but she worked hard at home because she was warm. Klara got wood for the stove from somewhere – I didn't ask about that either – so we could be warm in the evening, and Erich was very pleased with her. He said everyone else was using electricity so carelessly, and what would become of Anna? Well, we had different priorities.'

With the same mischief, almost tinged with malice, she told me that Erich had relented, and Anna had started drawing lessons. The woman was a friend of Ursula's, and came to Ursula's house to teach Anna. They kept it from Erich that the teacher had been pronounced decadent and forbidden to exhibit, and Anna made a few dull, representational drawings to show at home.

But another time she told me the city was laid out like a map at night, with the snow everywhere, making a mockery of the blackout. It was a tense calm, the phony war, a nerve-racking, irritating joke.

'John Watson,' says Donald. 'John Watson.'

'He said you wouldn't know him.'

'This is the code for Washington. I'd better try the number.'

He's going to the study. I don't want him in there. I've got all my herbalism laid out on the table, even my first piece of written work. I don't want him to see it.

He's sitting with the receiver against his face, staring at me with that look of bullish outrage that comes when he can't understand me and feels threatened. He's talking to whoever has answered the phone.

So there's no-one there called John Watson? Well, if they're sure – he repeats the number, she's evidently assuring him this is her own phone. Faintly, all the way from

Washington, a child's wails come out of the receiver. He apologises for disturbing the woman – I can hear her now, harassed, I can well imagine, by the conflicting claims of this insistent English voice and the crying baby. Who knows what is happening to it, while Donald keeps her talking?

Donald wants to know if I wrote the number down right?

'I read it back to him.'

'Bugger,' says Donald quietly.

'Donald,' I ask, 'what's going on?'

Again the bull stares at me, lowering his horns.

'I don't know. You took the call. If anyone knows, it's you. Are you sure you weren't dreaming?'

The troops got to the Somme, and there they stopped. 'Oh God,' said Klara, 'our poor boys. Now it will be the same as last time.'

Monika was in Berlin. She told me Helene went into her bedroom, when she knelt down with her arms on the bed and her head in her arms. Monika tried to comfort her, but Helene didn't respond. Her lips moved. Monika knew she was praying, and left her. Did Helene beg God to stop the war, to send the end of the world, anything, only not to stay there all-powerful and do nothing? Nothing. Did she get any answer?

A black-bordered letter came in the post: it was no consolation to learn that Jörgen had bought it this time, not Michael. How could it be? Trumpet calls announced the fall of Paris. Hitler said Germany's shame was wiped out. Helene and Monika wept together, and Klara shed a few tears for sympathy and old sorrow.

Monika said, 'They brought a division back to Berlin: it was Michael's. The Berliners forgot to be sceptical for once – Hitler hated them, you know – they went wild. They threw clouds of confetti at the soldiers and rained flowers on them. Goebbels greeted them from under a special triumphal arch. People thought the war was over now, because we couldn't see how England could hold out. Peace in a fortnight, plenty of people were predicting it.

'After the parade, Michael came to see us. He brought cigars – yes, he'd remembered to bring me some – silk stockings for us women – even Klara got a pair of silk stockings. He said Gustav was in Paris, lucky devil! Then he said poor Jorgen, he hadn't seen him since we'd all been at home together, but at least he'd died a gallant death. He didn't seem to want to let himself feel it. Helene stared at him, and he had to meet her eyes; his face looked terribly shocked, he went white. It was as if she'd shown him his own death.

'They left the silly triumphal arch up for months, and every time I came to Berlin it was shabbier and sadder. Then it was gone. It was quite clear it wouldn't be needed again in a hurry. The war had settled in.'

This is a queasy waiting game I'm playing with Donald: both of us so considerate, so careful of each other's feelings. In other words, we're walking a minefield, and we're frightened of explosions.

It was late August 1940, Berlin still (but only just) intact, when Helene watched an old man cutting a patch of hay in the midle of the city – no area too small to put to good use, and flowers feed nobody. It only took one old man to mow it. He was very thin, dressed in faded black, and Helene was frightened watching him, in case he missed his stroke and cut his leg off, but the grass fell in neat swathes, unmarked by blood or disaster.

14

Are those children playing or fighting? Playing, I think, though the fight could easily follow.

The point of the iron smooths the tuck of a skirt. The rhythm is hypnotic, but the job always makes my back ache. I ought to leave Donald his own trousers to do – why don't I? I'm frightened of explosions, that's why.

'Lizzie, it tickles!' My Sally with her high, excited laughter, her appetite for tickles and cuddles and kisses on the back of the neck. What is it I can hear now, coming out of the past? What Tante Maria heard from outside the bathroom door.

'Bernt, it tickles!'

He was disappointed in me, wasn't he, the little boy with his mop of black curls like Sally's. He said, 'It's all hidden, what you've got. I'm not hidden like that.'

I had a brother, so I knew what boys were like. I had expected the funny little dangling thing that I never envied (in spite of Freud) except when I'd wet my socks squatting in the open.

'Let me feel. Please?'

'No.'

I remember so well because when I was older I tried so hard to forget.

'Please, Karin.' He opened his black eyes wide and smiled at me, his head on one side. (Look at me, I'm adorable.) But it was curiosity that made me agree. I had put my own fingers in down there, what would it feel like with him?

He said, 'How odd. Everything you've got is so little.'

It felt different: more exciting, though less predictable. I had to giggle and shiver, and I said, 'Bernt, it tickles! It tickles, Bernt!' and jumped right away from him and bounced up and down to do something with what he'd let loose in me.

Maria got us sorted out, all right, re-establishing proper values. You can't have that sort of thing for free. It has to be bought by ironing trousers. Or can you?

There's the phone. Elisabeth has answered.

'Mum, it's Grandad.'

Now the jumping, dancing child is quite bewildered over

how to transform herself into the strong woman who can stand up to whatever he's phoned to accuse me of.

Defensively, 'How are you, Dad?'

'Karin, I want to know if you think I should come to this private view. Peter is quite adamant I should come.' Bewilderment isn't my monopoly after all.

Doesn't Peter know Dan will be there? Will I have to ring Dan to warn him? They avoided each other at the funeral: the ex-husband, the lover; each wanting to possess a memory without the other, annoyed to find it impossible. When Anna wanted to be no-one's possession.

In a pathetic voice, Dad continues, 'And you know what Edna's like, Karin, and I just can't, you know, at my age, I don't want to have that sort of strain between us. I mean, it's quite unreasonable of Edna, but you must understand, do you?'

He's frightened of me. That's ridiculous. Amazingly, I feel terribly sorry for the old man.

'Look, Dad, I haven't spoken to Peter, but what I think is that you should do just as you feel right. How are you otherwise?' (How do I mention Dan tactfully?)

'The thing is, Karin, I'd quite like to see your Mum's exhibition. Some of her work was at Abbot's Hall once, and I went in to Kendal and had a look, and once there was something at Carlisle, but I'd like to see them all –'

'I could send you a catalogue.' (In a plain cover, of course.)

'No, that's no good, because Edna would see that, and anyway, I could never come to London on my own, and she wouldn't come with me –'

'Couldn't you come and do London together, and you go to the private view on your own? Or some other time, maybe. The private view will be full of arty people talking their heads off.'

Is that too tactful? Not surprising that he wants to see what she accomplished when she left him. But Edna, sulking in a hotel room while he goes to the exhibition, or coming with him and making trite jealous comments – can't imagine what that's supposed to be a picture of, they're all overrated, if you ask me – no, that would wreck whatever he experienced.

'Well,' says Dad, 'I might get down to London some time before the exhibition goes off. Maybe I could come down and stay with you?'

I invite him without hesitation. We chat for a few more minutes. He confides that Edna is out shopping (which is why he can speak openly). I'm amazed at the things that have refrained, just for once (or could this last?) from coming between us.

I can date Helene's second breakdown by the final battle at Stalingrad. Michael was caught with the rest of the Sixth Army in the Stalingrad pocket on the twenty-second of November, 1942, and it was just afterwards that Helene woke up screaming, then began to cry, and didn't stop except to scream in terror again.

'Hitler's coming. He's coming to get us all. He's the Antichrist, the Beast –'

But Helene. You don't say such things.

Modern technology is undeniably wonderful. Not only does it allow you to exterminate millions of Jews and other pests, but it gives you the wherewithal to silence the screaming voice more effectively than with a threat or a gag. You can slug the mind itself, and then say the patient is calm.

I don't know if Uncle Robert was involved in the first raids on the German capital. I thought Granny Birkett told me a lot, in her sitting room with the sun coming through the net curtains and winking off Uncle Robert's medals, blinding off the glass so I had to move to see the photograph of himself beside his Lancaster bomber. She told me about the narrow escapes, the discomfort, the time he bailed out over Kent, and yet, when I look at what she told me, I find great white patches of nothing, like censored news items, but she didn't censor, she just forgot. Or did my own guiltiness about listening make *me* forgetful? In any case, I'm no longer inclined to make the RAF the main culprits, though there's no doubt they contributed to Helene's collapse.

Strange how ready Anna was to talk about the bombing, or maybe not. Those years she spent as an auxiliary air-raid warden, the days and nights she got through with so little sleep; they were her university, her proving ground. It was afterwards, in peacetime, that she experienced the full extent of the terror. Talking helped. And the fact that she survived it made her careless of other dangers. I'd forgotten that till now. (Dan said one day she'd electrocute herself. Well, she didn't do that.)

Monika showed me the letters from Berlin – she'd kept them. You could see them getting shorter and more breathless. There were things Monika knew through conversations that were more informative, because you had to be careful what you wrote: letters were opened. Monika knew her sister was crumbling, and made a lot of trips to Berlin, disguised as business, trying hard to prevent the inevitable. What was that story about Anna and the Swing-Clique? It'll come to me.

There are things I seem to know that may be fantasy, but I think I can be confident that they are the product of brief sentences I took in, of attitudes I absorbed, insecurities I took over. They are authenticated not only by Helene's eyes as I see them looking out of my own face in the mirror – so real I half expect my curly blonde hair to turn chestnut – but also by the memory of the nights when she sat beside me singing me to sleep, the touch – so vivid, even now – of the old dry hand on mine. The story becomes an act of love.

It's my imagination, as Edna used to say, damning it in her terms. But Anna taught me that imagination has its own truth, myths are the account of something more real than fact. If I'm mythmaking, so be it.

The cellar was lit by one yellow electric bulb, and it was difficult for the women to see their knitting. Anna had her sketch book, but she wasn't drawing in it, she was looking into a dark corner, her face stern, concentrated, remote.

Evening after evening it had been like this: the alarm went, they traipsed down the steps, complaining because they wanted to go to bed, chatted a little, were bored - life suspended for a while, and what was the point of it all? Another practice.

Frau Blumenthal sat in a corner, with Ilse and Elli coughing into a handkerchief, all of them tired and grey-faced. It was obvious Elli wasn't going to be able to keep up the pace at the factory much longer. Beside them, the sacking was decaying on the sandbags.

Listening for the All Clear, they heard the sound of engines overhead.

Frau Schenk said, 'They're ours.' She fumbled her Mother Cross, Helene reached for her rosary, then her eyes went to the Blumenthal women, and in her mind she saw Vati Blumenthal on the ground.

Erich said, 'They're flying very low.' He put one arm round Helene and the other round Anna, and the three of them clung together as the first bomb came down. They felt the blast that was relayed so faithfully and far by the Brandenburg sand - it struck them, like an invisible fist. Something was hit nearby. The dust flew in the shelter, and Elli wasn't the only one coughing now, though she was worst off. The shaking stopped, but the planes were still roaring overhead. Down came another lot of bombs: again the walls shook and the dust blew straight down their throats.

Anna looked round her and saw dusty faces expressionless with fear: she wondered if she looked like that. It occurred to her that the cellar would never survive a direct hit, and that was her worst moment, thinking they might be buried under all that earth and rubble, imprisoned forever out of reach of the sun and air. You could hear the guns in the distance, but the bombers kept coming. Another hit, and another, and then relative quiet.

Frau Schenk wailed, 'But Göring promised us we wouldn't be bombed!'

Erich muttered, 'Then go wave his promise at those things up there, and see if that makes any difference.'

'Over and over again,' lamented Frau Schenk, 'they said the enemy would never bomb German cities!'

Did the Blumenthal women move closer to the wall, fearful lest they should be blamed? They must have been so changed from the confident, well-off women they had once been; now they were filth, pests, their hands and nails stained from the labour in the munitions factory, allowed only in certain restricted areas, the relatives of a convict, a man who had been arrested and beaten up before their eyes.

Anna sat watching the yellow bulb swinging, its filament making crazy patterns as it bucked and bounced. Bits of plaster were coming down in showers from the ceiling. It was hell, having to sit still while every nerve demanded to be allowed to run, to get away. She looked at her mother, whose lips were moving and her hands shifting the rosary beads and shaking. (Helene told me God sometimes kept silent, and it was then you had to be faithful, however hard it might be.)

Then the All Clear sounded. Their hearts and lungs calmed slowly, though they felt a little light-headed. And they were closer to each other, more German, less cynical. Erich announced he was going to volunteer for air-raid protection duties. Helene didn't try to dissuade him.

They went back to bed, and later in the night she woke convinced she could hear the planes. She hadn't heard the warning. She woke Erich, who listened for a while, and said, 'No, Helene. You're imagining it. Please can I get some sleep?'

Frau Schenk was delighted when the *Luftwaffe* began to bomb London, putting Erich's components to good effect – but Anna insisted most people shrank from the gleeful pictures of destruction. She said, 'And your grandfather said it was senseless.' He said it was senseless, and he firewatched during the raids and helped clear up the damage afterwards, and got increasingly tired, yet he insisted on going to work to help make the senseless things that were going to be dropped on the British – perhaps because when there is nothing around you but senselessness, you might as well give up hunting for sense? Who can measure the damage wrought by millions of well-meaning people with a minimum of malice in their hearts?

Suddenly the raids virtually came to an end, less than two months after they had started. Other German cities were bombed, particularly in the Rhineland and the Ruhr, but the Berliners were able to sleep almost every night. London was still suffering, and the pictures came over and over again, in the papers, on the newsreel; Hitler's answer, that was going to deafen and blind the enemy. The enemy.

It's coming again, that tearing inside me, too brutal to be dismissed with words such as senseless. I want to whimper and cry and hide between the floorboards, but there is no hiding place, it's inside me, that orgy of mutual murder. Which leaves me forever a stranger, on the rack because someone's asked me to buy a red poppy at the door. Will the cracks come apart one day, will I fall to pieces? I always give them money, and refuse the poppy. They don't understand why. They look at me askance.

Helene said, 'When our troops were sent to invade Russia, we began to listen to the BBC so we could hear what the British said was going on. There were so many wild rumours. We kept it from Anna – but she found out in the end. Once we'd started, we had to keep on, it was as if the radio was a magnet. If we'd been caught, we could have been sent to prison. Later they shot people. We turned the volume right down, and unplugged the telephone in case that was tapped. All the same, I thought the walls turned to glass every time.'

One evening she met Frau Blumenthal and her daughters coming back from work. They had to wear the yellow star now. Frau Blumenthal stopped and told Helene they were moving, and she'd like to thank Helene for her neighbourliness. She said she was glad of this opportunity to say goodbye.

They were going to live with another Jewish family, and a Party official was moving into the apartment. Frau Blumenthal was jittery and kept looking round her. Helene said she hoped Frau Blumenthal would be happy where she was going, and Frau Blumenthal smiled a strained, ghastly smile.

'They say we may have to go and live in Poland,' she told Helene, who said, 'Oh, I hope not. So far away.' And no-one mentioned Herr Blumenthal, who may still have been in Sachsenhausen.

Helene said, 'Then Ursula came to the front door. She was on her way to visit me, and Frau Blumenthal told her the story over again. She kept repeating herself and jumping at little noises. Ursula said she was to come and visit, if she was in the area. If there was anything she could help with – and maybe that was why, later – you know. I've told you that. I can remember how a month later Frau Schenk came in shaking her umbrella and said the Jews were leaving, she'd seen thousands of them at Grunewald station. She wondered if the Blumenthals were among them. She said they'd be better off in Poland.'

(His blood be on us, said the Jews, and on our children. Was that the cause, the excuse? So many curly-haired black-eyed children dragged from their mothers and taken naked to the gas chambers, machine-gunned, starved in the interests of science. Where does it end? Is their blood on my children?)

Monika said, 'One of the things that broke her was Michael coming back from Russia, what they'd done to him out there.'

Monika was on another trip to Berlin, for her textile business, or spin-stuff as it was now clumsily but Germanically called.

'He sat there in their best room,' she said. 'He'd got thinner and coarse and cynical. He was laughing and joking about the war, boasting of how many Russkies he'd killed, he had brought Erich a bottle of vodka and got drunk on it himself. In her presence he asked Erich where the best girlie shows were, and made fun of Erich when Erich said he didn't know. Helene was staring at him as if she'd seen the gorgon. I shook my head at him; he noticed her.

'And then his eyes turned shifty, and his face collapsed. He said it was horrible what they were having to do out there, they'd re-opened the churches, yes, but when things were going on outside that would make Jesus weep – and Helene shuddered, but she actually looked better. He said, "I can tell you, we've got to win this war, because God help us if we lose, if they take their revenge on us for what we've done out there –" '

How was it for Jesus, when he wept, knowing there was nothing he could do? He might submit to violence, but that wouldn't save the Jewish temple.

' "I don't know if it's any consolation that the Ukrainians are worse even than the SS bastards. They're wild beasts: they'd do anything to the Jews and the partisans. Our chaps, even the SS, they're doing a job, some of them don't like it, but they get on with it, but it's pure pleasure for the Ukrainians –" '

But Jesus, Jesus wept, what sort of excuse is that, you didn't even get pleasure out of it?

'He said, "And it's so cold, you can't imagine it, we can't get the vehicles to move, and men are turning black with frostbite and dropping into the snow. Give me some more vodka. You can't fire your gun. It's minus thirty-six Centigrade. What sort of temperature is that to fight in? And no proper winter gear. You'd think *they* couldn't fight either, but they've got men, thousands of them, coming from God knows where – another glass, Erich." Erich had hardly touched the vodka. He looked round him and whispered, "We'll never capture Moscow." He said, "Helene, you like praying, you'd better pray all you can, that we don't lose, that I'm not damned –" '

Monika said she and Erich took Helene to the cinema to cheer her up. It was meant to be some harmless romance with no mention of war, only they'd changed the time of the newsreel. Russian corpses, to show how well the war was going.

'Helene said she was leaving. We said, "But Helene, the film's just about to start." She was talking too loudly. Everyone was looking at her. She said, "I've got to get out. I'm suffocating here." She let out a sort of gasping groan, "I can't get any air!" The main film was beginning, and someone shushed us from behind. People turned round and stared angrily. Helene didn't even know about them. She got up, fighting for breath. Her face was pulled quite out of shape. She didn't look like herself. Then a man behind said, "Let the lady through. She's ill." He stood up, too, and he was wearing SS uniform, death's-head and all. He made way for the three of us – people moved quickly then – he actually came out with us and asked if there was anything he could do. Very young, he was, and good-looking, his face all philanthropic concern. Blue eyes like a child's. He asked if she was asthmatic. Erich said yes, she was. He said we'd take her home, there was no need for help, we thanked the SS man for his kindness, and he went back to his evening's relaxation. Sugary sweet, that film would have been, with nothing about death in it.

'We walked home. Helene began to breathe more easily, but we were angry with her for making such a scene. I thought, look at her now, so calm; she did it on purpose. I asked her if she was worried about Michael, and she said, "God is silent. Why? How many more must die?" Erich said, "Helene, don't say that, not on the street!" Defeatist remarks, you know. She could have been thrown into prison. And then she said, "We'd better get the tram after all. There's going to be a raid." We were really scared of her, then. Why? There was the obvious reason: dangerous talk where anyone could hear her. That last remark could have got her shot as a spy. There was more to it than that, though, we felt she was right, and our skins crawled. We played at reassuring her, really we were like two children telling their mother it isn't bedtime. Worst was the feeling I had that she knew exactly what was going on in my head.

'We did take the tram. Erich was turning the key in the apartment door when the sirens started. After that, Erich told me, she always knew when there was going to be a raid, till they came so thick there was hardly any point in sheltering.'

The RAF was back, and would keep returning. One night, Helene wouldn't go to the cellar.

Anna said, 'She told me we'd go to church. I protested that there wouldn't be anyone there, and all she said was, "We've got time." So I went out with her along the street. The church was ten minutes away, and by the time we got there, the markers were falling. Christmas trees we called them, that's what they looked like, and they fell very slow and silvery and dignified and beautiful. The bombers were coming down low, almost touching the chimney pots. I thought the church door would be locked, but she opened it, and in we had to go. It was empty and echoing, you could smell the incense from Sunday. The windows rattled every time a bomb fell, and now and again a small pane popped out of its frame and smashed on the floor – once just by me. The RAF were opening the buildings with explosive, that's what they did, then they dropped the incendiaries to set them on fire. Your uncle was up there, perhaps. If he'd done his job better he'd have saved his mother and brother a great deal of trouble and anguish, wouldn't he?'

She laughed savagely; it hurt me. She went on, 'It might have been worth his life, mightn't it, to keep British blood pure? Well, my mother got her rosary out, and knelt down by the high altar. "Holy Mary, Mother of God, pray for us sinners, now and at the hour of our death." I looked up at the high vault and felt giddy, I thought it was going to come crashing down on our heads. I ran to my mother and put my arms round her, I wanted her to comfort me, I wanted it so much, but she kept praying, and I could see how she was gripping the rosary, as if she could squeeze something out of it, safety maybe? I don't know. And I knew we were on our own and she was more vulnerable than I was myself. All around us there was crashing and waves of blast shock and the rattle of flak, and her voice cracking – "Lamb of God, who takes away the sins of the world, grant us your peace." I told myself I was going to start firewatching. She could come here on her own if she liked, but I was never coming again. I knew then, I didn't believe in it. I knew it did no good, and I could do better than stand here helplessly waiting for death. I said, "Mutti, I'm going to start firewatching. Do you hear?" She just said, "Jesus, Lamb of God, who takes away the sins of the world –" I asked her again if she heard me, and she went on praying.'

And Erich, when he heard about this episode, said nothing. He didn't try to stop her sheltering in the church. Was that because he knew it would be pointless, or just because he was exhausted – long days of hard work in the factory, and I shall never know if he had concentration camp convicts or slave workers under him – or was it that he might even have been relieved to have her safely under a tombstone, and be able to weep normal tears for her? I couldn't blame him if he did, since that was how she felt about him in the end.

She refused to listen to the radio, on any channel. She began to have migraines, sometimes they lasted a week. Then Anna began to give cause for concern: summer 1942, she was just seventeen –

15

Someone at the door. Donald. He's home early. He wants to make a call to the States.

'Couldn't you have rung from work?'

'No. Don't ask questions.'

He's been in the study for almost an hour: I can't concentrate on this meal. Why do we have to have meat, all covered in blood? The children don't like it anyway.

Here he is again.

'Can't that child stop playing the fiddle? It's driving me crazy.'

'But Donald, you can't hear it in the study, surely?'

'I'm still on the line to the States. Do you want *me* to go up?'

So now I'm in a row with Sally that's far noisier than the violin practice, she doesn't want to stop, why should she, she's having a lovely time, I must hate her if I want her to stop.

'It's Daddy. He's on the phone.' And why was I so obedient?

'Then Daddy hates me. All right,' she screams so her voice cracks, 'I'll go up to the attic!'

Here's Donald pounding up the stairs, he says the phone call is over and everyone can make us much row as they like now. Sally picks up her violin and carries on playing.

The dinner is burned, the smell has come twisting all the way up the stairs and the whole house is full of it. It's horrible, it makes me think of charred corpses, and Donald says he doesn't care and he's going out to the pub to eat. I'm never going to eat meat again, or cook it, he can do that for himself, if he wants, along with all the other things he's doing that he doesn't want me to know about; what did you do in the peace, Daddy?

He doesn't like Sally's music. I expect he too has seen the resemblance. Besides, it makes her incalculable, beyond his control. He likes artists to be dead and safe. That was probably Hitler's reason for hating modern art and jazz – the fact that jazz was black people's music was secondary.

When Anna developed the taste for jazz – she never gave it up – it was a piece of dangerous subversion. She joined a Swing-Clique, meeting friends to read English books and listen to jazz on the BBC. Worse, Anna left the books around the flat for Klara to find, carelessly covered in brown paper, and listened to jazz on Klara's day off, with the windows open. Erich (Monika said) found her at it.

I can hear him, thundering at her in true patriarchal style (with the windows shut). Saying that she was endangering not only herself but her parents who could be punished for bringing her up to be so perverse. It wouldn't matter that she'd been digging people out of the rubble the night before, having progressed well beyond firewatching. Jazz was treason, forbidden books poison, and her associates all likely to end up in K3. Anna would listen sulkily, muttering that all she wanted to do was to enjoy herself – that she wasn't exactly having a wonderful youth, and why shouldn't she – casting a hostile glance at her mother's closed door.

And Erich, angrily, 'I can't help that.' Counting the cost, maybe, of the hard work he put in to keep her a political innocent.

In my mind, Anna says, still more sulkily, 'Anyway, you listen to the BBC, don't you?'

'No,' says Erich. I can see them staring at each other for a long time, and he's the one who drops his eyes.

Monika told me one of Anna's friends was picked up in September, and vanished into a camp, though nothing was done to his parents. Erich and Helene were terrified in case he'd given Anna's name to his interrogators. Monika managed another business trip to Berlin. She said Helene kept asking herself again and again what she might have done to protect Anna.

Then Helene vanished. She hadn't left the apartment for days, and they thought she'd made away with herself, till someone discovered the ration book was missing. She came back without it, and began to talk.

Monika said Helene didn't care what she said, so she took her into the bedroom and hoped the maid wasn't listening at the keyhole. 'She said she'd exposed her family, she'd had no right, but the woman was so thin – she said, "they're hardly allowed any food now, you know that, don't you?" I asked her what she was talking about, though I knew. She'd seen a woman with a child on the street, and they were both wearing the yellow star. She said the ration book fell out of her hand of itself, and she said to the woman, "You dropped this." And the woman thanked her.'

And did it make any difference, when the woman was struggling for the last inch of air in the gas chambers, that an Aryan woman with tormented eyes had once given her the means of getting a few days' food? Did she even dare use it?

She told Monika that if Michael died he was damned, and she with him; if she'd let him die of the 'flu as a child, he'd have gone straight to Jesus. She said the whole of Germany was damned, even the little children, who had been marked with the mark of the Beast – and she made a swastika in the air with her hand. She said she'd killed her mother. Over and over again, said Monika, the same things, like machine-gun fire – maybe it kept pace with the sounds in her brain – she also said every time she shut her eyes she saw Michael, sitting behind a gun and firing into the amorphous whiteness that spewed whining shells back at him.

When the sirens went, she stayed in her room, which was a relief no-one could admit to, because what would she have said in the shelter?

In the small hours of one cold morning, she woke screaming that Michael had been killed. She knew it, she said. He was dead. Dead. Dead. It was Hitler who had killed him, she screamed. Hitler knew where they lived, and was going to kill every one of them in turn. It took an hour before Erich could bring himself to call the doctor, and then only because her abuse of Hitler was so loud he thought other people in the house might hear it. She didn't go quietly, though Monika begged her to be obedient. They had to strait-jacket her to get her away.

Michael never came home. He may have died that night, or he may have been taken prisoner, and died in a Russian camp like eighty-five thousand others. Numbers, what do they mean?

Seeing Donald, smelling the beer on his breath, I find myself overcome by unappeasable rage. It's all coming up like a mushroom cloud now the children are in bed. I can scream myself hoarse, how dare he go out like that, leaving me to shovel up the shit as usual? And what the hell are these phone calls? Are the KGB after him or what? I'm beginning to think there's always a car parked outside, waiting –

And his eyes go furtively to the window, and there is a car outside. I'm laughing, and getting angrier as I laugh, telling him all that's wrong with him and his way of dealing with me, with us –

He in his turn is outraged, why am I attacking him like this? Who burned the food? He says he doesn't dare say a word to me, I'm such a harridan, and ageing too (etcetera, etcetera) and I was hinting once he might have someone in the States, yes, he has, and she's nicer than me and ten years younger –

So, I point out, in ten years' time she'll be the age I am now, but I suppose he'll have jettisoned her by then, and does she have orgasms, I enquire, or has she learned to suppress them?

'She never bothers me with such selfishness.'

I laugh, briefly. Donald seems unnerved. Finally he mutters that he's sorry, but after all, I attacked him, didn't I?

I feel so tired; is that a way of ducking out?

'I'm going to bed.'

'I'll come too.'

After all that, he can think of nothing but sex. Are we members of the same species, he and I? In the end, I can't stand his insistent rubbing against me any longer, and I open up to him. The sooner, the quicker it'll be over.

God, what a fool. I'm dry and tense, and he hurts, hurts, hurts, it feels as if the opening has shrunk and he's forcing me apart.

I do the garden, between-service maintenance on my car, small electrical repairs, decorating. Occasionally Donald helps. Added to which I clean, cook, clear up, iron. Occasionally he peels the potatoes or dries the dishes. I'm the one who can sort the children out. I'm a really capable woman, and I have a private income, which most really capable women don't have. Yet the children are certainly not his only hold on me. There is something else – I can't call it love, it doesn't feel tender. Maybe it's Meg. Was there ever a woman who hesitated to divorce her husband because she didn't want to lose her mother-in-law?

I used to say I wanted to model myself on Monika, but to do that I should have got into Donald's company and become the business manager. And when Monika got pregnant in 1937 she stayed at work, when she miscarried she was out of hospital and into the office. I, in the same position, sat at home and refused to see anyone for four weeks.

Making ribald jokes and laughing at them, drinking beer and staying slim, invariably elegant, she annoyed her daughter-in-law, Maria, while her low blood pressure and healthy lungs frustrated Josef because the endless cigars and cups of coffee should have been so bad for her. Klaus-Peter, on the other hand, a model of abstinence, died of a coronary the year I was born. He adored her, no question about that. Everyone loved Monika, even (reluctantly) poor Maria. I'd never have thought this before, because Monika was on the side of the angels – Sybille could be seen as a poor copy of Monika – the best Erich could manage. Physically of course there was no resemblance, but she was a businesswoman, sensual, rather loud. Still, widowers do marry their deceased wives' sisters, and if Helene had been tidily under a gravestone . . . he'd never have dared try, the way things were.

I couldn't have modelled myself on her. What a relief if I could have made myself so relaxed, so uncomplicated, so kindly and tough! I'd never have been afraid of becoming Helene.

When Mary began to scream in the library at Oxford, just before Schools, when they took her away and kept her in hospital and drugged her and gave her electric shocks, I saw everything I feared happening to my best friend – it was as if she took it for me. But it didn't take my fear away. I'd learned to lie, in my childhood. The outbursts other people noticed were moments of relief from the cramping dissimulation.

Most of the time I was the diplomat my father claimed I could never become. After Mary's breakdown I got better at it, worked to acquire camouflage, because I'd seen what they do to you, when you let your wounds show.

If there is a God (and something within me can't quite reject the concept) it must be a multi-faceted being, kind and cruel at once. I don't know if I want to talk to it.

Helene appeared to recover from her second breakdown, that is, she stopped screaming, so they sent her home.

'She wasn't her old self,' said Monika. She had left that woman a long way behind, a memory on a photograph, a face that looks out shyly next to small, serious Anna and the doll Mimi, flaxen-haired as her owner, who sits now in Sally's bedroom, having come through all those murderous years with the same fixed smile on her face.

Monika laughed bitterly and puffed at her cigar. 'I'd say it was the events of those years that put the finishing touches to it all, and it would be true, and yet what's also true is what I saw, from one day to the next.'

Monika said Klara the maid had gone to spend her night off with her sister in the workers' quarter of Wedding. The house got a direct hit, and Klara and her sister (or what was left of them) were dug out several hours later. It was February 1943, and though Uncle Robert was paying regular visits to Berlin, the worst was still to come.

It was a Sunday when someone brought the news to the apartment, and Helene was lying on the sofa with the beginnings of a migraine. Each wondered where they'd get another maid, with so many women having to work in the munitions factories, and their family wasn't the sort of deserving case young girls were sent to, the mothers with three or more young children and a husband at the Front. Anna herself would have been doing that sort of work if she wasn't an air-raid warden.

'We don't need a maid,' said Helene, sitting up. 'I'll do the work.'

'You?' Erich was quite outraged. Firstly, she was a *Gnädige*, a lady, not a scrubber of floors and black-leader of stoves. Secondly, she'd just caused all this trouble, being ill, had only that moment got off the sofa (with the beginnings of a migraine) and was offering to start the heavy work as if nothing had happened.

'Finally,' Monika said wickedly, 'he might have wondered if he'd end up having to help, and in those days that was unthinkable – you know, the moment he got in at the door your mother had to have his slippers ready for him. That's the way it was with my father. After all, men were the providers, that's what they told us. Except I provided for myself, and no-one brought me my slippers. At least I made sure Klaus-Peter got his own.' She cackled.

'Well, far be it from me to say housework should be the salvation of any woman – I don't believe that at all – but there are individual cases, and anyway, if it was between two women who should do the work, I don't see why the *Gnädige* shouldn't lend a hand. Helene was tireless. Quite tireless. Of course it wasn't just the housework she took on again. It was your mother, and Erich – she and he had been sleeping separately for some time, but now she had him in her bed with her again. I don't suppose she enjoyed anything but satisfaction that she'd done her duty, but that's been enough for a good many women.' Monika's face changed as she said this. She looked entirely stricken and hurried off to make coffee, refusing help. I have no idea what unhappy nerve she'd touched.

February 1943: there were almost two and a half years of the war's agony to go, the climax of the performance.

The apartment, Monika told me, was huge, far bigger than her own in Bad Godesberg. They shut some of the rooms off, but the ones they still lived in were terribly difficult to heat, even with the double glazing. One of the living room windows had been shattered by blast, so they had taken it out and nailed thick cardboard over instead. The kitchen was designed to waste a woman's time.

She was tireless. Well, I knew her like that, not as the elegant lady of the photographs, but with her grey hair tugged back into a bun, her long skirt kilted up, her sleeves rolled so she could get down to it. Acute depression paralyses, but if you are simply desperately unhappy, activity is as good a drug as any. I can remember Peter, his wrists stitched shut, making himself useful about the house, any job that came to hand, constantly on the move, and no doubt he worked as busily at the desk job they found him when he couldn't fly any more. I can feel it myself: you vacuum all the rubbish up from the floor, and you feel you've sorted your life out too. If I had unconditional faith in the activities that make employed people feel valuable, I'd say housebound women spend their lives looking for spiritual health in spurious quarters.

Look at Erich, who had a fetish – represented to me as a virtue – of getting to work on time, whatever difficulties lay in the way (like a burned-out tram, or the ruins of half a street), however little sleep he might have got the night before. He was one of thousands. After a raid, the obsessive cleaning-up began, even the opera house was put together again so the damage was hardly recognisable. That sort of thing was still possible at this stage. And thinking about it, I can see that this was simply the repetition, on a larger scale, of myself with the vacuum cleaner.

16

The phone. Strange squeaks and electronic noises: it's an intercontinental call.

'Karin Birkett.'

No answer, but something that might be a breath. Then the line goes dead, and I can hear a buzzing emptiness. Is it

117

the one who rang before, the fake John Watson? Who is he? Has he tried the office?

And there's a car parked outside, and a woman stitting in it, looking at a map. I'm almost hoping she'll stay put, that I'll catch her watching the front door, but she's starting the engine and driving away without even glancing in my direction. I'd better get my mind back down to herbalism, that ought to stave off paranoia.

1943: Stalingrad had been lost, the British were taking control of Libya, Morocco, Algeria. My father was somewhere (I never asked him) on the track that eventually led him to Berlin. Hope, if that's the right word, was trickling away like sand out of a fractured egg-timer. The sand had been turned for the British, but the Germans had enjoyed too much luck at the beginning of the war, and had squandered the lot. So Erich knew, who muttered fiercely to Helene, 'We should have made peace instead of invading Russia. We should have ended it all then. God knows he should never have started it at all, but once it had begun, that was the moment, and he trampled it in the Ukrainian mud, God rot him. He should try to make peace now, even now it might work.' And when Mussolini fell, and Italy negotiated with the Allies, Erich muttered, 'And why doesn't it happen here, what idiots we all are to let ourselves be goose-stepped into a fool's grave.'

Well, he said that, but he didn't do anything about it, which was why he was able to convince the Gestapo the following July, when someone tried. He told Anna after the war that it wasn't what they might do to him, but his wife and child he was afraid for. Easily said, and as easily dismissed if you've always been able to say what you like without looking round first.

Twenty-second of November: they didn't expect a raid, with Berlin shrouded in milky fog. But if you want to obliterate a city, you don't need to see much detail. Uncle Robert and colleagues were thwarted, however. Unlike Hamburg, Berlin didn't become one annihilating firestorm.

The houses were built of stone, not wood, and the wide streets acted as firebreaks. Even so, there seemed to Anna to be plenty of fire.

'My coat floated up above my head and my hair stood on end with the heat,' she said. 'The air was alive with dancing sparks. The asphalt was like soft hot mud under your feet and you could see the street lamps bending over, the smoke got into your air passages, but fortunately I had a handkerchief – that did some good, not much. You felt other people dying all around you. The boundary between life and death seemed hazy, so one minute you thought you were dead yourself, the next you were surprised you were still alive. Omi came out, too, but there wasn't much any of us could do.'

Buckets of water against an inferno, and what is it like to be burned to death? The rabid Nazi, the pensioner, the policeman, the small child, the soldier on leave and the unborn baby in the mother's encircling womb. Others were smashed up by the rubble of their tumbling houses. I don't suppose Uncle Robert had time to think about any of that. He had the technical details to see to, and his own life to worry about, which was to end a few days later when a *Jäger* got him after all. Granny Birkett told me that when he came on leave he had been dreadfully tired. He slept, woke briefly, and slept again. Maybe he told himself he was only doing his job, and wasn't enjoying it either. Or maybe he thought he was in the air above a nest of noisome cockroaches.

There was little respite for the bombers or the bombed. There was another raid the very next night and then three days later. That was the night Uncle Robert's plane went spinning downwards in flames, onto Berlin in flames, nothing but scorching and gradations of heat and flames from sweating to shrivelling. I think that was the night a land mine flattened the house Ursula lived in. It wasn't a direct hit, and the people in the cellar were saved, but Ursula and Hedwig never went to the cellar. Helene helped dig for them.

Anna said your hands used to get filthy and sore and full of splinters. You had to pick up brick after brick, so slowly in case anyone was still alive, you mustn't damage them by causing a landslide. It was raining on the city, each drop laden with soot, like mourning, like tears.

Brusquely, Anna told me, 'We found Hedwig after an hour. She was quite dead, but almost in one piece. Then we found someone we weren't expecting. It was Frau Blumenthal, dead. Ten minutes later we came on the daughters, crushed in each other's arms. It was another hour before we found Ursula. She was a horrible sight. Frankly, she was meat from the breast downwards. My mother was sick. My father and I had seen worse, and we weren't.'

So that was the end of the female Blumenthals. They were killed by the RAF who were fighting (so Granny Birkett said, so the history book said) on their behalf. It was Ursula's fault. If she hadn't taken them in, they would have been in a camp, where they could have been killed by Germans, in the proper way.

'So then,' said Helene, fetching out her handkerchief, 'we knew why they never took shelter, because if the house was hit and the Blumenthals were found, Ursula would have been in trouble. She might have been shot. You see, by then there weren't supposed to be any Jews left in Berlin.'

And Anna, 'Well, she had no family. She and Hedwig, they decided to take the risk together. It was easier for them.' I heard hostility in her voice.

'Didn't you like her, Anna?'

Ursula had introduced her to her drawing teacher.

Anna said, 'She was a strange woman, in many ways. But she was good to Omi. You can't imagine what it meant to Omi, to lose her like that.'

Nervously, I suggested, 'She must have known something, to take the risk.'

Anna, irritably, 'I don't know what she knew, or what she thought might happen to them. There were rumours and whispers – you believed them, or you didn't. How were we to know what was true? A lot of what you heard wasn't.'

And still I persisted, 'Well, she was a heroine, wasn't she, and so was Hedwig. Aren't you proud to have known women who had so much courage?'

'*Ach was*, courage. It means different things to different people. I've got work to do. Haven't you?'

Her cynicism so often made it hard for me to believe in anything, though it didn't proof me against the biggest and most persistent illusion of all. And yet she went to Greenham, my mother took her cynicism to the fence at Greenham, and was arrested there.

Silence and whispering can become habitual, maybe even shut off whole areas of the brain and memory, leaving only the still picture of what you permitted yourself to see at the time – the editing may be final. Impossible, then, even to look at the shadows on the edge of the picture and imagine what they might represent.

Anna's voice says, 'It didn't do any good, did it, anyway? They died all the same, and Ursula and Hedwig with them. Five people instead of three. And they would have been found out sooner or later, if that hadn't happened.' She wouldn't have said that to her friend Sabine. She never said it at all, yet the words sound so convincing I could believe they were a memory.

'There was hardly time to mourn,' said Helene to me. 'You had no time to think. The bombs came down every night, later it was night and day, and all you thought about was staying alive, doing what you could, and clearing up afterwards. It was a blessing that you couldn't think. And your grandfather had his work to go to, and Anna was taking her Matura exams, but she never knew the results, because all the papers were destroyed in a raid.'

Still nothing in the post from Germany. Does that mean Bernt's forbearance has limits, or is he wondering what to write to me? I don't want to think about it.

It was a blessing that she couldn't think. About, for example, the fact that even Josef had been caught up and was with the army in the East, beating the long retreat. Because the gas had just been cut off for the last time, and she was going to have to scrape about and find out where she could get a tiny electric hotplate on the black market – it would cost an astronomical sum, but that had to be found. Straw shoes, ersatz coffee, cereal sausages could be coped with. You had to be able to cook. When there had been a big raid, the water pressure wouldn't supply the first floor, so she would carry a bucket downstairs, wait in the queue to fill it, and drag it up again, carefully, so the water didn't start rocking and jump right out of the bucket, wasting your effort and aching arms. She preferred not to remember that it wasn't going to get any better. Germany was beaten, whatever anyone did, which was why Erich now tolerated the black market.

Work and raids by day, and broken sleep and raids by night. You were so tired, thought would have taken a lot of effort. You endured.

She remembered walking home past rows of blackened ruins, clutching the hotplate wrapped in brown paper – and the porcelain stoves hanging on the walls, shivering in the falling sleet. You had to watch your feet, because of broken glass. There, up against a heap of earth and rags and rubble, stood an angry knot of people, screaming and rowing over who had pushed whom, threatening each other with relatives in the Party, two grey-faced women and three exhausted men. And then the sirens began, and they all bolted together into what seemed to be a cellar, only the flight of steps was blocked halfway down by rubble. Well, it was better there than out in the open. You could already hear the planes.

'They left that late, didn't they?' muttered one of the men. Helene thought, please God, don't let me be buried in here, because I'd lose the hotplate.

And the first bomb fell, in their ear, it seemed, and their mouths were all of a sudden full of dirt. A frightened rat leaped out of a hole in the staircase. Helene remembered it, hopping like a kangaroo, with its young in its mouth, and one of the women gave a little scream, but no-one moved, and the mother rat went back twice, and removed two more pink babies. While the bombs fell close by, all but demolishing the wall they were huddled against. They clutched each other (but Helene kept hold of the hotplate), someone saying, 'Breathe in and out steadily, that's the way to keep calm.' One of the men began coughing desperately. His wife said his lungs had been wrecked by gas in the First War, and the dust in his face . . . The other woman, who had been screaming abuse at him up there, gave him the scarf from her head to protect his mouth. 'God bless you,' said the wife.

'We were close, in those months,' Helene said, 'so close, Karin. I don't think we'd ever loved each other so dearly, the three of us.'

She said sometimes the snow sizzled on the hot stones, after a raid.

17

I'm going to scream. I can't. It hurts too much. I can't – he's gagging me with his mouth. No sound would come out anyway. No-one would hear. I've got to make a noise.

'Karin! What the hell –?'

'It hurts too much. Get out of me.'

'What's wrong with you?'

Why am I afraid to tell him? Damn it, I'm articulate normally, more articulate than he is, yet I feel I shan't be able to convince him.

'It's because I don't want you. If I was a man, I wouldn't be able to get it up. As it is, I don't want to let you in.'

I've said it. I feel stronger, and yet scarily lonely.

'Pass me my pyjamas, then.' He sounds sad and depressed. I hand them over from where he threw them down, and put my nightie on, pulling it right down over my bottom. That feels better. He asks, 'Is it because of Martha?'

'Is that her name? No. It's more than that. It's you.'

He switches his bedside light on. My eyes crimp up against the glare.

'Donald,' I say, 'can we talk this through?' This is it, the positive approach that might open out the blind alley.

'What do you want to talk about?' And his voice says, there you are, if you've really got anything sensible behind all these vapourings, let's have it.

I say it's not going to happen in a minute. He answers that he's going to America in a fortnight, and his preparations for that will keep him very busy. So I say it depends how important our relationship is to him, and he says he doesn't see how a lot of talking can do much good. He says I need to change my attitude. I hate people who talk about attitudes. They never want to change their own.

'In other words,' I say angrily, 'you think my feelings are rubbish.' Yet it's as if I need his permission for them. How did I get into this?

'You're like my mother.' (Well, I wasn't expecting that.) 'I think you both get a kick out of dredging up all sorts of things you ought to leave alone, with her it's tapeworms, and with you it's just anything. You've no respect for anyone's privacy.'

I wanted his permission to exist: the faint contempt he always had for me proved his power to legitimate me.

'It's you that's the problem,' says Donald. 'So what is there to talk about? I haven't the time. I haven't a private income. Your mother should never have left you the money, if you'd had to earn your living there wouldn't be time for all this brooding. I wish you'd snap out of it.'

He says, 'Do you know what time of night it is? Can't we go to sleep?'

He says, 'Why can't we have a normal marriage, like other people do?'

He's probably right, I am the problem. We were fine together till I moved out of alignment and spoilt the fit.

Instead of planning my readjustment, I push his foot out of my half of the bed – fortunately it's queen size – and use the dark to take me back to Berlin.

There everything was falling to pieces, but Helene's marriage remained perfect until January 1945, when Erich was sent with the Berlin *Volkssturm*, the Home Guard, to hold the line of the Oder against the Russians.

She said, 'Every time we were together in the evening, every hour we spent together, it was as if we'd reached a safe island in the middle of a raging flood, and that was all that mattered, you had to make it all that mattered, you couldn't have borne to think of what was all around you. When any minute the sirens might go, and you were out in the waters again.'

I can see them, sitting round a table as close to the porcelain stove as they could get it, eating scanty food they had all queued to get. (If you saw a queue you joined it: there was bound to be something useful at the end.) The electric light dimmed and rose uneasily. Often it went out altogether, and they had to use a candle.

Anna told me, 'She wouldn't let us talk about the war, or the bombing, while we were eating, she said it would ruin our digestion.' Sometimes they went to the theatre. They needed distraction, or they wouldn't have been able to save lives.

Yes, save lives. When you dig a child out alive, is it really not worth remembering because the child has blonde hair? Admittedly, Erich was making armaments. He also put out fires.

Karl was with the troops in Norway, but he was about to be captured. Gustav was still in France, finding it less and less of a pleasure trip. Josef was still alive (as far as they knew) being pushed nearer and nearer to the East German border.

Helene said, 'One day, Frau Schenk's apartment was burgled during an air-raid. It was between two and four in the afternoon, a lovely blue day, but the sky was ploughed with the Americans' vapour trails. The burglars were very tidy, and they took all the food and all the valuables. She called on everyone in the block to complain – she was convinced it was the French workers, because she said they were natural thieves. She said it was quite shameful that this should happen to her with her Mother Cross, and five children, and her husband at the Front, and her eldest son so important in the Hitler Youth. Poor lad, he probably died on a rooftop in the last battle, and he was only just sixteen. Maybe she thought if she told everyone about it, it would turn out to have been a bad dream. We gave her what food we could, but she never found her jewellery. They didn't get the Mother Cross, because she was wearing it.

'She believed everything they told her. I can hear her saying the night was always darkest before the dawn. She tried to organise a rota of people listening for the air-raid warnings on the radio, that way we'd know when the first Allied aircraft crossed the frontiers. By then, they'd landed in Normandy, so there wasn't so far to go. She managed to get one family to join her, and they drove each other mad.'

There was a day when Anna passed a group of children playing with something on the street.

'I didn't take much notice, because that was the sort of thing they played with nowadays, shrapnel, pieces of aircraft – they used to scavenge, too. I wasn't above looking for parachute silk myself, but for painting, not clothes, you got such a nice effect. I don't know what made me look again, when I'd almost passed them, and I realised they had a bomb. I walked towards them and told them to leave it alone. They wouldn't. We stood there, arguing, and suddenly it struck me that the thing might go off any moment, and none of us was seriously frightened. I only wanted to move them because I knew in my head it was the right thing to do. I grabbed two of them, little ones, and dragged them away. They thumped me and swore at me. Then the bomb went off. I was far enough away only to be blown along the street, but the rest of the children were dead or dying, and there were other people hurt, who hadn't realised what was going on. I did what I

126

could. When the ambulances came they told me to go home and rest. Omi put me to bed, but the sirens went half an hour later, so I went out. I couldn't stand it in the cellar.'

It was the twentieth of July 1944 that Klaus Graf Schenk von Stauffenberg left a time-bomb in a briefcase beside Hitler and walked off to make a telephone call. Only someone moved the briefcase. Helene said they never knew who scribbled the note that appeared under the door, warning them that they were about to be arrested. It gave them a little time. They used it. Anna went off to stay with a friend. Erich and Helene went over their movements of the last few days: innocent enough, because they really weren't involved. The only lie they would tell concerned Anna. They would say they had no idea where she was, she had gone out and hadn't returned, and they hoped she hadn't been killed in a raid. When the knock came on the door they were listening to the late-night broadcast Hitler made himself, so everyone should believe he was alive.

'At the Prinz-Albrechtstrasse,' said Omi, 'they split us up. I didn't know what was happening to Erich. They questioned me for hours, it was exhausting, but the worst thing was the sense of what was happening to other people, what they might do to us – you saw things, and heard things – no, I don't want to tell you what, Karin, that sort of thing is best forgotten. It was worse for your grandfather, because of what they'd done to him before. I remember saying over and over again how important his job was, and what a waste of their time to arrest us for nothing, holding up vital war production. I think his employers put pressure on them. We were lucky. They let us out.'

Then she said, 'It made you feel very tired to think – not that I want anyone's death under normal circumstances – to think the war might have ended then, to think what we might have been spared.'

No Russian invasion, no rapes, maybe no Berlin wall, her marriage saved perhaps, thousands less deaths. But a few births wouldn't have happened either: my own, Peter's, our children's.

She told me there were allotments in town that summer, growing potatoes and tomatoes and white-flowered beans, and people built themselves cottages against the walls of ruins, and hung curtains at the little windows. Some of them were destroyed before the inhabitants could move in. And her geraniums bloomed on the balcony, but she took no cuttings when autumn came.

'I felt it was the last summer,' she said, 'that no more summers would come, darkness would fall and last for ever. So I enjoyed this sunshine today, at this moment, for who knew if I'd be alive in a few hours? This meal I was sharing with my family, the feel of my loved ones this minute, this sacred bread on my tongue in the sidechapel – because by now, the rest of the church was a ruin.'

The bees must have buzzed in and out of the bean-flowers that summer, just as they do any year. But there were other things buzzing: flies in the increasing, barely tolerable heat, and a hot dry wind blew up dust and nasty smells, smarted in your eyes and prickled your face. The year reared up like the last standing wall of a building on a hillside – you couldn't recognise what was behind the empty window holes.

She said, 'There were clear, still days, in September. The year held the summer as if it would never pass, the leaves coloured a little at the edges, a few fell off. I wished time could stop then, before the frosts. Tante Marlene died, and I was glad for her. She'd stood enough already.'

In October, Erich was called up along with every other male between sixteen and sixty. He was part of the *Volkssturm*, the Home Guard, who, the government assured the people, were a weapon of last resort that would probably never be needed. Did Erich laugh savagely? Once he told me about it, I don't know why. He was interested in Peter, not much in me. He said he had to find time to drill, in the middle of his duties at the factory and his civil defence work, and they were more interested in training the recruits to give the Nazi salute properly than in anything useful. They were given sticks instead of guns, and were allowed, just once, to hold a bazooka. He was disgusted, but he had to go. Himmler had warned anyone thinking of deserting that their families would be summarily shot.

Germany was shrinking.

Anna said, 'My uncle Gustav died in the Ardennes offensive in December. My stepgrandmother got the telegram while she was closing the house up. She and Hanna were coming West because they didn't want to stay for the Russians. They buried their valuables in the garden, thinking they'd go back – I suppose Polish people dug them up. Your grandfather couldn't get out of going to the Front now, his factory had run out of raw material and closed down.'

He was in his late fifties, and not very well fed, in spite of the black market. All the same, he must have been tougher than Helene thought, or he'd never have survived captivity.

She said, 'I'd unravelled some old jumpers and knitted him new ones to keep warm, because it was January and his chest was weak, and I found a few special things for him to eat. I put them in his bag and I thought I was laying them in his coffin.'

She said, 'I looked round at the room, and everything in it hurt me as if it was poisoned. I felt I was wounded to death. He told me he couldn't bear to go, either. He said he was hurting, and he begged me to take care of myself and Anna.'

As if her vigilance could deflect bombs and shield from fire and blast, as if safety were an act of the will. You mustn't disturb these delusions, or life would become intolerable. Well, why doesn't it become intolerable? Why don't we all go out on the streets and riot against what is called real life?

Erich was going to the war because if he didn't, he and his family would be shot. He didn't really think he could do anything to protect them, but when there's nothing you can do that's effective, you have to do something, or go mad, and they'd had enough of that in the family. He left. It seemed too soon. All that might have been said wasn't said, and yet at the same time they could say nothing that meant anything, feeling only a dull certainty that the parting had already happened, and needed separation to ratify it. Along with this went the conviction that he might turn at the corner of the road, and come back –

He left. A week later, the stepmother arrived with Hanna. 'They had walked all the way,' said Anna, 'hiding in ditches from bombers and planes that shot at them, with other refugees who almost trampled them underfoot when they slipped in the frozen mud. How my stepgrandmother got there, I don't know. She was dying of pneumonia. She was worn out with years of hustle and childbearing. It didn't take long.'

She said, 'Hanna had her cremated; most of the cemeteries had been ruined. Then someone told her the coffin in the crematorium was always empty nowadays, to save materials and labour, they were burning the dead in batches and scooping out indiscriminate boxfuls of ashes to give the relatives. They saved the coffin for the next funeral. I can see her now, looking at the cardboard box – you couldn't get urns – wondering how many people were in there. She was a widow. She'd married her fiancé when he was called up in 1939, and he was killed in Poland. No children. Someone told her to cheer up, at least her mother wouldn't be lonely where she was.'

The Communists were coming out at night to daub 'STALIN IS WINNING!' and 'DOWN WITH HITLER!' on the walls of the underground in red paint. If the message was unfinished, you knew they'd been caught and summarily strung up. Once Helene was waiting at a tram stop (because she was so tired she didn't mind waiting God knew how long for one of the few trams that hadn't been burned out), and she felt a corpse's feet tap her on the shoulder. She hadn't even noticed it. Then she was afraid to look in case it might be someone she knew.

While crazed optimists repeated Goebbel's promises of secret weapons, the Americans carpet-bombed the city. Afterwards, there were so many corpses they were stacked up on the streets, on either side of the people walking to work. I found the photograph in a book. They look relaxed, as if they were asleep, especially the children with their arms thrown out. They must have done their best to make the stacks tidy, but there's nothing tidy about violent death, no matter what you do with the remains. (Auschwitz, Berlin, Warsaw, Hamburg, Coventry, Dresden, Hiroshima.) So, what else is new? Heaps of corpses, that sort of thing is boring, banal. (Kampuchea, Iraq, Iran, Kurdistan, East Timor, El Salvador, Argentina.) If it happens outside Europe we can still claim we've had forty years of peace.

18

What a diabolical noise people make all standing and talking at once. My ears get confused and refuse to tell me what anyone's saying. And I don't like champagne. Keep your head down, Karin, in a couple of hours it will all be over. Hell, half these people aren't even looking at her pictures – nor are they interested in the artful nibbles with their bits of smoked salmon and olives and tiny perched salads – they're after the drink, and looking for the right people to bore.

Ah. Here is my sister-in-law.

'Karin! How are you? You look wonderful!'

'Ruth, how nice to see you, you look wonderful too.'

Correct openings on both sides. You can never find out whether Ruth really likes you, but she puts it across well. That journalist is tracking Peter now, which is the only reason Peter's still talking to Dan. And Dan knows that: I can read it on his face. What did I say to the journalist myself? I can put this conversation with Ruth on auto-pilot.

'No, I got them both when we went to Singapore last year, the blouse and the trousers, yes, much cheaper to buy silk over there, and have it made up . . .' (No, I know she was perfectly happy when she did the collage. You can see from the colours, can't you? We all went out to dinner afterwards and had a wonderful time. Yes, in the kitchen, with the children sticking fabric onto paper beside her.) 'And I do like your earrings, Ruth.' (Yes, of course I'm pleased to see her work here. I think the gallery is lucky to be able to hold the exhibition. What do I like best? Oh, I think the photograph of what she did on the fence, at Greenham.) 'And the children, how are they?'

'They're very well, we've just sent them to a convent school, it costs an arm and a leg of course, but we're doing all right with the bookshop these days.'

The story of the eighties – for the well-off. Let no-one imagine Peter and Ruth running an antiquarian bookshop, or some eager affair full of books on social problems and radical thinking: Peter and Ruth have marketing strategies and blockbusters, and they look at any book in terms of sales figures.

Here are Peter and Dan, tailed by the journalist. I find I'm delighted to see Dan, who puts his arm round me and annoys Peter by kissing me as well. I reciprocate. He's always flirted with me, quite harmlessly, and Peter has always hated to see it.

'Karin, you're beautiful.'

'So are you, Dan.' He raises an amused, complicit eyebrow at me. His hair is still thick, though quite silver, and he is elegantly shabby, wearing sandals today, in contrast to Peter who has definitely overdressed – why did he wear a suit?

'I've come from a business meeting.' Peter explains, pulling his jacket off. 'God, it's hot in here.'

Peter has stayed blond and beautiful, the slight bitterness in his face adding a touch of piquancy, and Ruth is a picture of dark smartness; you could take her anywhere. Even the dangling feathery earrings are well within the limit of what is acceptable.

Peter says, 'Why did they have to put that photograph of the Greenham thing in? And her statement in court. It's bad enough that it happened, let alone publish it to the whole world.'

I say, 'I was proud of her.'

'Oh yes, you went to court, didn't you? I couldn't have stood it, seeing her in the dock.' Spoken with passion.

'She was wonderful, wasn't she, Dan?'

'Yes. The photograph enlarged brilliantly, too.'

This is Anna's occasion, and I, her mother's daughter, am there to hold her flag. Closer than anyone, even Dan, though he cares almost as much as for an exhibition of his own sculpture.

Peter asks, 'Where's Donald?'

'Coming. He has a meeting in London too. It must have run over.'

Peter likes Donald, so he's hoping he'll show soon. I'm not. Peter discharges his duty as uncle by asking about my children, makes critical enquiry about my course in herbalism. I respond in kind and show a polite interest in the form of technology Ruth and he are busily introducing into their shop, their home, their children's heads – but no-one will see wires sticking out, it's all microchips nowadays. Just as long as I (intolerant puritan) can keep myself from asking if Julian, Emma and Henry really need a computer each. I tell them about Sally's violin lessons and Elisabeth's riding, and they make counter-claims about their own children's achievements – I don't want to talk about this, we might be anywhere.

'Dan, I want to look at that photograph again. Would you come with me?'

I've been rude. Peter's face tells me so, and I can read his expression, telling Ruth it's no more than he expects of me, strange woman that I am. And Dan, just as bad as myself.

Anna took the photograph the minute she finished, before the police noticed what she was doing and arrived to stop it. It took just half an hour, because she thought it out at home and numbered each piece of fabric that she attached to the wire, all those different-coloured flapping tongues making a design worth including in this exhibition. It must have been even better, moving in the wind.

'Defacing the fence,' says Dan beside me. He laughs.

It was a grey cold day. She'd gone there on her own. She'd never have gone when there were crowds, and they'd recently cut the number of police, so there were only a few women to watch her. She passed the camera to another woman before her arrest, and press-released the photographs.

Her statement:

'My name is Anna Schäfer. I have two children and five grandchildren, and I was born in 1925 in Berlin. I am a professional painter. Some of my work has been purchased by this nation to hang in our major art galleries.

I am charged with defacing this fence. You have seen the bundle of rags which the prosecution has labelled 'defacement'. I would like to show you the photograph of what I made. I spent as many hours planning this creative work as I spent on the paintings that were purchased for the British nation.'

(Schäfer passed the photograph to the magistrates.)

'Why did I make this picture on the fence at Greenham? Because everything I produce is made against the background of the threat that Greenham represents, and could all be destroyed far more quickly than the police destroyed my work. The missiles stationed at that base are designed to save us (so we are told) from conquest by the Russians. We are expected, should deterrence fail, and it looks very likely that it may, to be pleased to be dead rather than to endure this fate. I think I am probably the only person in this room who has experienced conquest by the Russians. I can tell you that I did not prefer death. Those who did and committed suicide are forgotten, and those who tried to take their nation with them have been properly condemned by history as madmen.

'I have endured obliteration bombing, and I can tell you that I preferred conquest. So did many others. I have endured starvation, chaos, total breakdown of all social systems, military rule, living in the rubble with the stink of rotting corpses – all that has given me some small idea of what it would be like to survive a nuclear war.

'After the war, my prayer was that my children should not grow up in fear, as I did. They grew up under the threat of nuclear war, and now my grandchildren look like being the last generation. We are closer to the end of the world as we know it than we have ever been, and no-one can calculate the consequences.

'I did not deface the fence: I mitigated the way the fence is defacing the countryside. I made the fence beautiful, and the police removed the beauty as soon as I had finished, but (addressing her arresting officer) at least you let me finish. Thank you.

'If you fine me, I shall not pay. I am prepared to go to prison. Thank you for listening.'

The verdict: guilty. She was given an absolute discharge. No action was taken when she refused to pay the twenty-five pounds costs.

She stood there in the witness box, her clear voice with its slight German accent dominating the courtroom, her short hair white and untidy, her face bony-beautiful, her eyes severe with the authority of years of disciplined looking within and outside herself –

'Go on, cry,' says Dan, putting his arm round me again. 'I'll make sure no-one disturbs you.'

'I'd better not. It'd show on my face afterwards.'

'Your brother's hardly looked at anything,' mutters Dan angrily.

'What do you expect? You know he always hated her work.'

'Did he refuse the profits, when she died?'

'He thought if he hadn't got what he wanted of her, he might as well collar the money.' He gives my shoulder a squeeze, and lets go.

I put the champagne down on the floor and grab some orange juice from a passing tray; it helps to drink something. Oh, God, Donald has come. He's talking to Peter, and has seen me cuddling up to Dan. And he doesn't like Dan – outraged morality?

This is a new part of the gallery, and has the sharp irritating smell you so often find in new buildings. Donald seems absorbed with Peter now. No doubt they're talking about profit margins. No; he's also looking round the room, checking that the pictures I loaned are there (by kind permission of Dr Karin Birkett) and he sees the fabric collage. So that's done.

Another art critic – a less offensive one – makes polite noises at me, interspersed with shop-talk at Dan, technicalities about the pictures, and remarks about the fabric collage. She's trying to find out if Anna planned to do more of that sort of work, though it was in some sense, wasn't it, a development of this – she indicates the photograph of the fence – though this, being politically motivated, couldn't be in the same league.

'Couldn't it?' I ask.

Donald barges in, 'So you gave them that thing. I'm surprised anyone thought it was worth exhibiting.' He points to the collage. The art critic looks delightedly, maliciously amused.

Dan says, 'If you kept your mouth shut, Donald, you'd make less of a fool of yourself.' He always had a temper. He used to leave the house shouting while Anna retreated behind the slammed studio door. The rows kept the distance they both needed, that Anna especially needed.

'Oh, forget it,' says Donald.

Right now I love Dan, but if he'd ever moved in with Anna, he could have destroyed her work. She knew that. She didn't sacrifice her integrity to love, she valued what she was worth.

Donald says, 'I thought you'd destroyed it.'

'Why did you think that?'

'Because of the associations.'

'I couldn't kill the last thing she did.'

'That means you think I killed her.'

We are walking past the Houses of Parliament, almost at the tube.

'I don't think you killed her, Donald. She died in a motorway accident.'

A black car, containing some VIP, emerges from parts forbidden to the public.

'Why didn't you tell me you'd kept it? Why did you wait for me to see it today? No, don't answer.'

I don't. Because now we've got it in the open there is nothing for us to say to each other, and nowhere to go, which is maybe why our feet keep going so busily, as if to make up.

Sitting in the train at Paddington, opposite me (Intercity plastic comfort), he speaks.

'I'll move out, shall I?'

'We'll have to explain it to the children.'

The unhappy, fearful look comes into his eyes.

'Can you do that? And I won't fight you for them. You've more time for them.'

'I'll want to stay in the house. I'll buy you out.'

'I'll take Steve's flat. You know he's going to the States for a year. He hasn't got round to looking for a tenant yet. I think he'd let me move in right away. The sooner I go, the better, eh?'

It'll be a divorcee's den, since Steve's wife threw him out a year ago. How neat, how tidy. It's almost frightening how easily it seems to be working out.

I hope they believed me, that it's not their fault. They must know I understand how they're feeling. I'd far rather they blamed me than blamed themselves. You suffer today and torment tomorrow. I had a miserable childhood, snivels the rapist to his dead victim. Is there any escape?

Elisabeth: 'I knew it was going to happen. I'm not as stupid as you think.'

Sally: nothing. Ran off to her room and I couldn't hear the violin. She's had me up three times tonight, but she won't wake out of the nightmares: they subside, and there's a respite. My sleep's been disturbed too many times. I might as well accept wakefulness. Sooner or later, maybe half-dreaming, I'll be back in Berlin.

I don't know if I can believe in the ways out offered by religion. I haven't the baggage for those journeys. (Perhaps I need a few more rebirths.)

I'm here, stretching my limbs as I need in the bed. It's cool and quiet in the room. After so much unrecognised loneliness, it's good to be simply alone.

19

I find her queueing – there was a rumour that the shop had sausages. You couldn't see anything from the window, crossed as it was by wide planks of wood to keep looters out. It was open for two hours three afternoons a week. You couldn't even see the shop from where she was standing.

A woman, nervy-looking as they all were from lack of sleep and everything else, whispered to her friend behind Helene, 'Hey, have you heard this one? How long will it take the Russians to conquer Berlin?'

'I don't know, how long will it take?' The friend gave a little hysterical titter.

It was a shivery day towards the end of March, and the gunfire wasn't far away. The ruinous wall alongside had once been a house, and a nice one, too.

Helene's fingers were on the rosary, 'Holy Mary, Mother of God . . .'

'I'll tell you. Just two hours and five minutes.'

'Why two hours and five minutes?'

Nobody moved when the siren sounded. A faint shudder ran through them, no more. Who was going to lose their place in the queue for a raid?

'Well, when they see our barricades, they'll hold their sides laughing for two hours, and then it'll take them five minutes to get over them.'

The two women shared brief, embittered laughter.

'Ach, it's our fault,' said the first woman. Helene stared at her big wrists. She was bony and large and her skin was loose where the fat had been. 'We were too well off, we were always complaining, and now look what's going to happen to us, we'll spend the rest of our lives as slaves.'

'. . . Now and at the hour of our death.' She looked at her own fingers, swollen now with hard work, washing and scrubbing, and she herself oh so thin, and now and again her sense of smell sharpened, and distressed her with the realisation that she and everyone else in the queue smelt high for want of soap and water. Only this gave her comfort, not the beads she held, not the images, but the certainty born of the words, this thing called God, the thing I can't quite dismiss. Supposing it lives inside us, and there is no choice between belief and disbelief, only between war and reconciliation? Supposing there is no escape?

She said the planes were RAF Mosquitoes built of wood, designed to annoy rather than devastate, but lethal enough if you were in the wrong place at the wrong time. The queue shrank against the wall, while hell burst out around them. They escaped by good fortune, or a miracle, or whatever you call it. A baby started to scream, but the mother stuffed her breast into its mouth. Helene thought: yes, people are still having babies. That one's really young.

It might have been an hour they cowered there, not much of a raid at all. Some of them were nipped by debris, but it seems no-one was so badly hurt the others could have moved up the queue. The sirens sounded the All Clear. They began to dust themselves off, and talk again.

'No, not in our block. The water's completely gone. You have to get it all out of the old street pump.'

'Too bad.'

The queue shuffled forward. There was a one-legged man complaining about the shortage of bunkers. His wife had been in a cellar three years ago, and it got a direct hit. He came out of the field hospital to find himself a widower, and his children dead.

'Listen, chum,' said a woman. 'You be glad you don't have to worry about what the Russians might do to her.' (But Helene never said that was rape.)

And the woman who had told the joke asked, 'Do you think it's quicker if you cut your wrists downwards or crosswise?'

'. . . Pray for us sinners.' She wasn't going to take that course now. And Erich had been taken prisoner by the Russians. He was out of the fighting, and might come back.

The joking woman's friend, having given the hysterical, whinnying titter again, started to talk about ways of making cakes without fat, if you had cod-liver oil.

'Cakes!' said the one-legged man. 'Hark at her. Cakes! If I can keep body and soul together, that's enough for me, never mind the frills.'

But children were still having birthdays, and First Communions, especially now, so many were getting their First Communion now, before the Russians came. The queue began to unravel from the front, and the word came down the line: 'Sold out!'

'*Verflucht!*' said the one-legged man, but none of the women swore. They set out, patient and dogged, to search for another queue that might be more productive.

'Frau Schenk?' said Anna. 'She killed herself.' (Leaving her four daughters aged eighteen, fourteen, twelve and ten unprotected and to the mercy of the Russian pricks.) 'She threw herself out of the fourth-floor window, and there was all the mess to clear up on the street. Her son went in his Hitler Youth uniform to look for a coffin, but they said they were all finished, and he'd better get a big paper bag to stow her remains in.'

By then the Russians were in the east of the city, refugees still cluttering up the streets, shells falling instead of bombs, and German soldiers were fleeing into Berlin, many of them throwing down their arms as they went. My grandmother, my mother, and my great aunt sat in the apartment, while the other people in the house hid in the cellar. This was a crazy way to behave, and somewhere at the edge of their minds they knew it.

Helene said, 'We had a pile of wood in the kitchen, some paraffin, a few buckets of water and a rough brick stove that could easily have set the house on fire. Every now and again one of us would go in there and make weak ersatz coffee with a few grains of sugar. We could taste it. For meals we had thin squares of the last loaf of bread. There was a pot of jam on one of the shelves, and we spent a lot of time talking about whether we should open it.'

Beyond the cardboard covering the windows, the noise was getting louder, and they were experienced enough to recognise the sound of houses collapsing, but they stayed put. Anna had said she'd go mad in the cellar. They puffed emaciated roll-ups to keep their nerves numb, even Helene. Helene prayed, Hanna joined in, and Anna was respectfully silent.

Helene said, 'I thought, this could be my death. But it had been like that so many times before, I couldn't get excited about it. I prayed as I breathed – it must have been like that for Hanna – I wasn't asking for safety.'

'What did you pray?' I asked her. .

'I don't remember.'

When the guns fell silent, they thought the Russians were coming. It was then that they heard the knocking at the front door, but it could have been going on for some time.

'It's them,' said Hanna, beginning to cry. 'It's the Russians. They'll kill us.'

Helene said, 'It's not the Russians.' And of course it wasn't. When the Russians came they gave the door much more of a whacking.

They opened up, and there was Josef, staggering with pain and exhaustion, in a uniform and without a gun. His light brown hair was soaking with sweat, and the threshold was wet with his blood.

He said, 'I knew someone would be at home.'

Between them, Helene and Anna picked Josef up and brought him into the living room, where they laid him down on the floor. Helene went for the water, thanking God they had been so careful with it. And this was a simple unecstatic act: she thanked God, she said, as she might have thanked anyone, matter-of-factly. She fetched a clean towel from the waterless bathroom and washed Josef's wound. His leg had been slashed by a piece of debris and the gash was quite dirty. Fortunately she had salt to dissolve in the water. He had been hurt in the next street, and had managed to get here. Again he said he had known there would be someone at home.

He wasn't tall, and his round face made him look younger than his age. Helene decided the best thing to do was to release him from the army. She told Anna to fetch some of Erich's clothes – it was a good thing Erich too was short – and Anna needed no further information. They communicated without words. Of course now they had no option but to stay put. I doubt if they thought twice about it.

They make so much of the courage of soldiers, but whoever talks about the courage of women, when the soldiers have done no good? She burned his army uniform in the stove, he protested a little, and then gave up.

He never lost his respect and admiration for her, though his wife didn't share it. Yet it was Helene who saved him for Maria, his childhood sweetheart, who was quite cut off from him at this stage, already under British occupation in the Rhineland.

Josef said, 'They dragged a mattress into the room for me. They were all sleeping in there by then, close to each other. She was so strong, your grandmother, her arms were really wiry, I'd never have thought it of her. I fell asleep, or passed out, I don't know which. I woke up and everything was quiet. There was only your mother in the room with me. A few minutes later your grandmother came in with Tante Hanna, up to their elbows in blood – I thought they'd been fighting, till I saw the dripping chunks of meat. Then they told me a horse had been killed by a splinter in the street, and everyone was out there carving it up. The fighting had gone into the distance, and no-one knew if we were conquered or not, but really all we cared about was eating that horseflesh. With the porridge and chocolate out of my pack, coffee to drink and cigarettes to smoke, we were happy.'

He woke up the next morning to hear the sound of battle outside, strips of light showing round the edge of the cardboard in the windows, while the plaster mouldings on the ceiling shook every couple of minutes at the impact of a shell somewhere, but never on that house. He was too dazed to remember that they ought to have been in the cellar. Part of a flower fell out of the moulding round the light rose. He lay there trying to will it back into place. He was feverish that morning, either because of the wound or some germ he'd picked up.

He could hear Hanna say quietly, 'He's getting worse, do you think we're going to lose him?'

Helene said, 'I'm not going to let him go.'

As if it was in any way up to her; she was to find out soon just how powerless her love was.

Outside the Hitler Youth and the SS sharpshooters were holding out, true to their oath. He said the shots sounded like death rattles. This must have been the twenty-eighth of April, the day I read somewhere that the Russians reached Charlottenburg. Hitler had two days of life left, the war had nine to go.

It can't have been the first lot of Russians who abducted my mother. They were decent enough, said Josef. They sent the whole family down to the cellar without showing much interest in Josef, whose obvious fever gave him an excuse for being ill – no need to mention his wound. And Anna didn't go mad after all, in that airless, terrifying underground retreat, while above them the Hitler Youth died, true to the lies that had been told them, senselessly and to no purpose. The battle passed over them, and went ahead of them.

No, it must have been the next wave, the ones who seemed

to be the lineal descendants of Genghis Khan (so my grandmother said). Slit-eyed, terrifyingly foreign, given to washing their hands in toilet bowls (I thought there was no more water?) with their wrists festooned with six people's wristwatches – you gave them whatever they demanded as quickly as you could, before they had time to shoot you – they were the Russian hordes of Cold War legend (but she never mentioned rape).

'It was the second lot of Russians,' said Josef, 'that drove us out of the cellar and onto the streets. I call them streets – ours was one of the few you could still give that name to. We had to pick our way through rubble and armoured cars, and every now and then we trod on a corpse by accident.' He shuddered. 'The battle was still going on a kilometre or so away, shells were flying, and you thought you'd lose your hearing with the noise. I was so weak I could hardly walk. I had one of the women on either side of me, supporting me, and the third one always resting, walking behind me, till it was her turn.' (Then the third one was still with them.) 'We staggered along, looking for another cellar. The first place we stopped, they wouldn't take me in: leave him outside, they told the women. They guessed I'd been a soldier, and they were frightened the SS would come back and shoot the lot of them for harbouring a deserter. So we had to keep going. It was twilight, but light came from the battle in the West.

'When we did find a cellar, we had half an hour's rest before the Russians came and turned us out of that place, too. They said they needed it for their wounded. I couldn't stand any more. Your grandmother put me over her shoulder and carried me – yes, I still don't know how she did it. At the next corner we found a cellar crammed with people. She made them let me in. How? I don't remember. I was too ill. They got water from the pump – someone must have queued for hours in the open – and sat up all night, sponging me to bring down the fever. How they had the courage, after all that had happened that day, why your grandmother didn't just lie down and die –'

Now I think I know. The strength with which Helene lifted her nephew came from the cussed determination not to lose this one, at least, perhaps not even to recognise what had happened to herself. She kept herself alive and sane because she had Josef to protect. The Russians had put their wounded into the cellar and taken Anna in exchange. Josef's memories were censored, but he didn't spare me the pain.

They used her like a toilet, in the intervals of the battle.

That's all I know, and lying here in the emotional nakedness of the small hours, it seems to me that I always knew it, and was always trying to escape. It came to me through the cord. It's our common whirlpool. It's swallowed women for thousands and thousands of years. It is our punishment.

They threw her down, ripped her clothes, and forced her legs apart.

I can't move. There's a feeling of panic in my genitals – I'm so vulnerable, we're all so vulnerable. And in some horrible, flesh-crawling way, my own sensuality comes shamed and servile to be whipped. You want to open your legs? We'll open them for you.

Oh, God.

My mother's body, the sanctuary, violated. (So there is no sanctuary.)

They were in the battle line. Perhaps she even hoped a shell would blow her to pieces? If she wasn't in pieces already. Humiliation, fear, and hard rough hands, and hard cocks shoving into her. Their faces above her, their panting breath on her, the sore agony between her legs because she was raw where her hymen had been split. (She couldn't push them away.) I can't stand it. It's not right. Why? Why? She was fourteen when the war started, seventeen when Russia was invaded. But it's pointless to think of innocence and guilt, when a Russian commander could describe it as a bit of fun. (And yet Bernt said, almost timidly, 'I don't want to hurt you.')

'In the end,' she once said to me, 'survival is a far stronger instinct than you'd believe possible.'

She survived. There's a roomful of paintings at the Tate to prove it.

Yes, I can say that, but these are words.

That memory of Bernt's gentleness is the hardest to take. It stops me hating them all. (And my father? Do I want to hate him? Do I?) I can't hate them all, not without losing whatever fragments of integrity I possess. It's lonely in the dark.

In the back of the armoured car, behind the windows they were shooting from, clutching the body she couldn't defend, dread giving way eventually to numb patience, it must have been lonelier still.

A pair of owls call and answer. Where have I been? With her? The word prayer comes into my mind, but I used no words.

She did survive. They failed. She was battered, but she kept the space inside her inviolate. Never in her life was anyone able to enter that sanctuary. Or there would be no roomful of paintings at the Tate.

She survived, that time.

Here is Sally, burrowing her way in beside me, kicking me, warm to touch, seeking comfort and giving it as she settles back to sleep in the curve of my body. The first birds are beginning to sing.

But Helene, even if she and Hanna escaped rape, had to spend that time in agony, knowing her child must be crying for her and getting no help, blaming herself for not protecting her, relieved only by the need to care for Josef, to find food, to stay alive. And when Anna came back to her, and she knew what had been done to the child, when she had to find the doctor for the abortion, there was still no time to allow herself to deal with it all.

20

The phone. Meg. Does she blame me? Please, Meg, no.

'Darling, I wanted you to know you're still my daughter.'
Oh Meg, I love you.

They run away from me, when they cry in the daytime. Usually, they take the cat.

The phone. Dad.

'Karin, Edna's sister's hip-joint operation has come up at last, and she wants to go over to her for a few days. Could I come to stay with you? We could make that trip to London we talked about.'

Conspiracy in his voice: I suppose Edna is about the house. Dare I agree? What will it be like, having him around? Will he blame me? I'll test him out.

'There's one thing you should know, Dad. Donald and I are splitting.' Silence. Surely he didn't misunderstand? 'We're getting divorced.'

He says he's sorry. He sounds gentle and concerned. He wonders if I can cope with him under the circumstances, he'll try not to be a nuisance, he says, but if I need support –

I say no, I'll be glad for him to come. I'm sure he won't be a nuisance. I can meet his train tomorrow, no problem, the children will come too, the Volvo has plenty of room for luggage (I'll have to get rid of it, though, it drinks petrol).

He's sold this trip to Edna on the grounds that, like a child, he's not fit to be left in the house on his own. Amusing.

Less amusing if he thinks Donald traded me in for a younger model.

'What happened?' he asks.

I turn from the kettle to face him, the tea tin in my hand. I'm not quite sure what he means.

'The divorce.'

Well, I thought so. At least I had time to think of an answer.

'It came to an end.'

Two spoonsful in a small pot. He doesn't like teabags and mugs. I'll have camomile; I need to keep calm. He eyes the dangling tag and the teabag with amused distaste.

'Very German.'

'The herbal tea?'

'Your grandmother drank it, years before it became a fad over here.'

One eyebrow raised, his face engagingly crooked. Oh, he's got charm, my father, just like Donald. I have to smile back.

'Well, why not?'

A pause. He doesn't want to answer, maybe because my voice is calm, maybe because he's lost interest in baiting me. Instead, he remarks, 'I didn't like him.' Didn't he? But I don't want to demonise Donald.

'We're trying not to get antagonistic.'

'Don't you feel it?' His voice is harsh.

'Yes, but he's the children's father.'

'Yes, I know. Are you going to be able to stay here?'

'I hope so. I'm looking round for a lodger. I've let the colleges know I'd take a postgraduate woman student. You know I'm not badly off. I may well get some part-time tutoring, but I'm doing this course in medical herbalism. That'll take four years, but I hope I'll support myself that way in the end.'

What will Donald say when he finds out – as he will – that I'm taking up the tutoring option after all? I don't care.

'Very organised.' What hangs in the air is: just like your mother. I don't want him to say it.

The cat comes in and rubs herself round his legs; animals always like him. He stoops to rub her striped back.

He wants to go to London tomorrow. Fortunately, he's keen to go alone.

He told me to meet him at the barrier, 'Don't waste money on platform tickets.' The children stand with me, inspecting the stream of people, and announce his approach. He looks really tired today.

I kiss the hard, shaven cheek and he gives me a peck in return.

'Well, what did you think?'

'I thought a lot.' He smiles grimly. 'I'll talk to you about it later, when they're in bed.'

Sally demands, 'Did you see the one we helped Grandma to make?' I explain. He says yes, he did. I'll have to take the children some time, it's their right.

'I like this room,' says Dad, looking round him. 'Uncluttered. Lovely bowl.'

'Mary made it, Elisabeth's godmother.'

Reflectively, 'You've got a good sense of colour and composition. Still playing the guitar?'

'Yes.'

The cat leaps on my lap, almost knocking my coffee all over me, then starts pushing down with her paws and claws. There's no way of stopping it; I'll have to shove her off. She retreats to the oriental rug Anna bequeathed me, washing herself and looking pointedly away from me.

'You've offended her,' says Dad, grinning.

'Too bad. Did you like the paintings?'

'Yes.'

Silence, except for the passing of cars and the song of birds in the garden. The cat gets up and strolls out through the open French windows.

He frowns. 'What she did at Greenham. I thought it was terrible, at the time. When Peter told me about it I was really angry.' He scratches his chin and crosses his legs. 'I told you I thought a lot. I mean, it wasn't just that I read what she had to say about it. It was my own anger. At the time, I thought – you're not going to like this.'

'Go on.'

There is a band of red sunset-light across the wall. You can see how the paint has bleached, round where the paintings usually hang.

'Well, what I thought was, bloody German, coming here and telling us how to run our country. I mean, that was what I thought then.' I keep quiet. He goes on, 'I mean, I really thought she ought to leave if she couldn't keep our laws. Oh, you'll say she was a British citizen, but I thought that was through me, wasn't it?' Another long pause. This is really difficult. I want to shelter behind my guitar, but I know I mustn't.

'I know what she meant,' he says, 'about what it was like to live in the ruins with the stench of rotting corpses. I mean, it was unbelievable. We thought we'd been badly hit in the war, the only way you could deal with what we'd done to their cities was to believe they deserved it. That wasn't hard. They taught us to hate in the Army, they said the only good German was a dead German, they said there was something wrong with every one of them, some flaw in their make-up. Then there were the camps. I didn't want your mother to be German at all, but it didn't work. Or with you. Peter, he was a different kettle of fish, and I always blamed your mother for what happened to him, but today I realised I hadn't helped him either.'

He looks so bewildered, as if he's only just understood what he's been doing all his life.

'Maybe I shouldn't have married her. No, but you see I didn't want to be like the rest of them with their German girls, buying them with chocolate and cigarettes – no, it wasn't just that. I really felt I couldn't live without her. But I rejected what she came from – we never finished the war, the two of us. Part of me still feels the same. I'm better off with Edna. And that man she picked up later –'

'Dan.'

'He was Irish, wasn't he? From Dublin, originally? I suppose he didn't fight in the war, then.'

I shake my head.

'Do you like him?'

'Yes, very much. I don't understand him. We live in different worlds. You know he never lived with us, don't you?'

'Yes. Marriage wasn't what she needed. But she was so young, and she'd been through so much – did she ever tell you she was raped?'

'No. I found out, recently.'

He watches my face in silence.

I've got to ask it. 'Did she tell you any details?'

'Just that it was a gang of them. She didn't want to dwell on it, and I couldn't blame her.'

Another long pause.

'Getting chilly, isn't it?'

Reluctantly, I get up and shut the windows, turning the key, locking us away from the air.

He says, 'I won't pretend I didn't sleep with her. She got into trouble with that, later, before she came over here, some prisoners-of-war came back and wanted to shave her head. I can remember a name – Schenk, that was it. Then they put him away because he'd been a Nazi.'

Another pause.

'Sometimes she got the horrors, and I just had to hold her. She never said anything then, she seemed glad to have me near her.' He sighs.

'Dad, what was it like?'

'I told you – almost everything was wrecked. And I was so surprised to find I was still alive, and in Berlin, where my brother was killed, I was drunk with it – do you understand that? No, I don't suppose you could. Most of the Germans were living in cellars, but your grandmother still had her apartment, and she let out the rooms. There was a family in each one. Her own family had the living room, with the stove, but nothing except cardboard in the windows. And she was really tough, in those days – I was scared of her, to tell you the truth. They used to go out to the countryside to barter for food – I gave them some, of course. You can't believe the sort of things they were eating. Your great aunt Hanna had a cache of reels of cotton, that a Russian had thrown her after the battle when he broke open a shop. She sold those for cigarettes – that was the only currency. Your grandmother ripped up old sweaters and knitted them up for her family.'

'She did that after the war too, with jumpers I'd outgrown. I can remember that curly ball of wool.'

'Yes. The bread was ninety per cent sawdust, and blew their stomachs up like balloons. I can see your mother now, in triumph because she'd found a clump of nettles for soup. She'd actually been after plants to make colours for her portraits. She said she hated them, and I got to understand why – she showed me something of what she could really do. Your cousin Josef got her the first clients, he had a job as a waiter in an army restaurant. That was really good because of the scraps he could bring home, but he was desperate to get back to the Rhine and see what had happened to his girl. Then he heard from her. That was the first time he smiled at me or spoke to me. Maybe he thought the British had raped her, too.

'Anyway, about October 1945 they were told to get out of the flat. Some British official was bringing his wife over, and they wanted it for her. On her own. There were about forty people living in that apartment then – four bedrooms, the dining room, the maid's quarters, big rooms. I got something done about it, but I don't fool myself. All it meant was my girl and her family got off, and someone else was turned out. I didn't feel sorry for the other people. They were Germans. Anna was different.'

Again, he sighs, stretches his legs out, rucks up the oriental rug, and pulls his heels back. He bends down to smooth the rug.

He says, 'Maybe you get in a mess if you mix people. We had to fight. But afterwards – I was on a station once when a refugee train came into Berlin. The people were from Silesia, where your grandmother was born. Old people, women and children, packed standing in open-topped trucks. It was winter, and most of the children and old people were dead. But as for your mother's answer, we've got to have defences. The only way is to make the price of war too high.'

'And if there's an accident, or someone tries their toys out?'

'Karin, I don't want to argue. We've done enough of that in the past. It hasn't got us anywhere, has it?'

'No.'

'I do want to say, I respect your mother's courage, now. I know how she hated getting involved. You've no idea what it must have cost her to let herself be arrested. Your image of a policeman isn't anything like hers was.'

'No, I do know, they handed it down to me. I never trust anyone who thinks it's their job to control me.'

He laughs. 'I know. You wore Edna out. She used to go to bed for a day when Peter and you went away. That's why I never understood why you went and married Donald.'

'To belong, of course. Why else? I thought I'd marry into Britain. I did what you wanted, Dad. It didn't work.'

'Hard words. I don't say you're wrong. And what about your children?'

'Do you mean I should regret producing them? As you regretted producing me?'

He looks distressed. 'I didn't. It's the pain you've experienced, both of you. I regret that. For God's sake, don't imagine I've ever wished you weren't there.'

What can I say? He's disarmed me, left me silly, weepy.

He says, smiling bitterly, 'I remember when I brought your mother home. She stayed the two nights before the wedding in the bungalow with Gran – well, the first meal Gran cooked her, Anna was sick. I tried to explain to your Gran that it was our food that was too rich for Anna. Gran couldn't believe that, she thought she'd been starving on her rations, and she'd read in the newspapers that the Germans were doing better than we were. She thought it was an insult to her cooking. Then she decided Anna must be pregnant, and not by me either, since we'd been apart for a whole year. I don't know which of them was more relieved when the two nights were up.'

'You were happy, at first?'

'I thought I was in heaven.'

'Have you ever been in heaven with Edna?'

'No, but I haven't been in hell either.'

The wind blows down the platform, and the end of the train narrows into the distance. I'm feeling bereft. I wish the children weren't at school.

I might never see him again. If that turned out to be so, I'd be very glad of these past three days, the long talk on the second night, the walk round the colleges yesterday, the quiet lunch together in the pub.

I'm sobbing, but without tears. I'd better get out of here. He's gone. Well, life cuts people off from each other no less bitterly than death does, and more quickly too.

After all, Helene grew old, could no longer be told what was on my mind, since it would have appalled her, started to complain about my short tight skirts and make-up, while boys had to be sneaked in quietly, if at all. It wasn't just the sight of her, so different from anyone else's relatives, with her prayer book and the National Health spectacles held together with a safety pin, her thin old legs bare and covered with varicose veins, though my adolescent irritability put those things first. It was that conflict between my own young sexuality and her horror of it; it was Helene, who I loved, who tried to foist shame on me. With that went the resentment I'd always felt because she came between myself and Anna. She was available to be resented as Anna was not. I fantasised a relationship with Anna that was perfect. I thought I'd get nurture from Anna, if Omi wasn't in the way. And so, when Omi died, I felt I'd wished her death, felt too that my unsatisfactory relationship with Anna was the pay-off for my wickedness. I couldn't mourn her properly because I thought

I was responsible for her death on the bathroom floor.

And why did she have to die like that, just under the toilet bowl, next to the toilet brush? She'd never have chosen to end her life there, never in a thousand years. Her face was snapping into ugly grimaces, distorting into demonic leers as if the features themselves had been changed. I stood there in stupid horror. She shouldn't have been there at all, she'd had a coronary and was supposed to be using a bedpan.

'Get the doctor,' said Anna, struggling with the jerking body.

I rang the doctor's number: he was out on call. The woman at the end of the line said she'd bleep him, then she said he'd just come in. I waited for him to pick up the phone, explained to him, begged him to come quickly. He said he'd leave at once. I went upstairs and she was dead.

She should have had a beautiful death, after all she'd been through she shouldn't have been finished off in such grotesque violence, she who was so gentle. It was as if the universe itself was mocking us for our delusions about what anyone deserved. Deserved?

At least she didn't die in hospital, among strangers speaking an incomprehensible language, who would have treated her as an idiot. She had Anna to care for her, and myself at weekends. She wanted no more.

The phone. Jane Nibbs wants a babysitter.

'I'm sorry, Jane, I'm coming off the list. I'm separated from Donald.' The next definition in the sequence: I'm engaged, I'm married, I'm having a baby. Sometimes people are shocked, sometimes there's a touch of *schadenfreude*.

Back to the cooking.

Edna. What the hell is she ringing for? Well, of course, it must be Dad. Oh, God.

'How's Dad?' I scarcely dare ask.

'He's all right. He's out.'

So what is it? Didn't I look after him properly? No meat, is that what she wants an explanation for?

'Karen, I've just found out that he really went to stay with you to see your Mam's exhibition. I found the catalogue and he couldn't keep it from me.' Oh, Dad. Dropped yourself right in it. 'What I want to know is, why did he have to keep it secret from me?' She's not angry. She's miserable.

'He thought you'd be upset.' I sound stupid.

'I don't understand, he seems to think I'm so jealous I can't bear to hear her name mentioned, why should I mind him going to see her pictures?'

I've been colluding with him. Who is she, then, when it seems I've been living with a false image of her all these years?

'I mean, your Mam's dead, isn't she, Karen? How could I be jealous of her, and anyway she didn't make him happy, and I have.' Quickly, anxiously: 'I hope that doesn't hurt your feelings?'

'No.'

'You say he didn't want to upset me, but he's upset me now, not telling me. He seems to think I'm completely daft. I mean, I wonder what's been going on between us all these years. He doesn't seem to know what I'm like at all.'

'Edna, stop, listen to me.' It's come to me what I must say. 'It's not you, it's him. Of course you make him happy. I know that. He's the one who couldn't bear to hear her name mentioned, he's the one who wanted everything she did out of the house, but he doesn't want to admit it, even to himself.'

She probably wanted her own children, and they never arrived. It must have been hard having two wild creatures like Peter and myself to cook for and clean after, to be taken for granted and despised by Peter, and hated and despised by myself.

She says, 'Thanks, Karen.'

Quickly, emotionally, I say, 'I don't think I've ever been fair to you, Edna. I'm sorry.'

Pause (shock?). Then, 'Don't worry about it, love. Nice of

you to say so. And I'm sorry about your marriage. Are you all right, down there?'

She says, if there's anything they can do to help, I'm to ring up. Her kindness is as unsettling as Donald's nastiness. Where will it all end?

And there goes the phone again. This is too much. I hope it's a telephone salesperson, then I can snarl at her/him.

'Hello?' I sound really unfriendly: good.

A quiet male voice, accented, tentative: 'I'd like to speak to Karin Birkett.'

'This is me, Bernt.'

I feel like an overstrung fiddle: something structural might give. He's in London (in London?) co-leading a course at the Harris Centre – have I heard of it? Vaguely, it's some holistic place, of course. He doesn't have to be back in Germany till Sunday evening (why does he explain it all so carefully?) and he'd like to meet me at the weekend, when he can talk to me about my grandmother. (And I thought a letter would be hard to deal with.) I ask him if he has anything in mind, he says his course finishes Friday at noon, and he very much wants to see Anna's exhibition. Would I be able to take him round it? Then we could have dinner together? He sounds hesitant, he's clearly not sure how I'll react to this last suggestion. I say that would mean getting back to Oxford quite late.

Con: I don't feel I can cope with this.

Pro: he obviously knows something about Omi.

Con: I don't like the idea that Donald and Bernt might be relieving each other like Mr Wet and Mr Dry – I won't attempt to decide who is who.

Pro: hearing his voice rouses a certain interest – but maybe this ought to be a con.

Cautiously, he says, 'I know it's difficult for you with the children, or would Donald mind looking after them on his own?' (Of course, he doesn't know how much Donald knows.)

'Donald's in America.' (This is true enough.)

'Does that mean you couldn't get up here at all? I could come to Oxford. What I thought was, I'm staying in the Centre, and I could get you a room too, but –'

Damn it, I will go to London. With all the risks and ambiguities of the encounter. I want to hear anything he knows. I want to see what he has become.

I think aloud. This is myself, after all, the mother endlessly making arrangements for her children. Since Friday happens to be the day their school is closed for the teachers' in-service training, I shall have to find some tolerant friends' mothers who'll have them all day as well as overnight. Or wait – there's Mary – he remembers Mary, doesn't she, she was in Heidelberg? She's Elisabeth's godmother, her eldest and youngest are the same age as mine, with one in between (the age the miscarried child would have been.) She's become a semi-professional potter, she works from home, and lives near a tube station in London. The children love her. Of course, it depends if she's got a craft fair coming up. (I'm keeping my feelers alert for signs of impatience, but I don't get any signals. Am I pleased?)

21

The sun strikes back warm from the steps, but I'm not relaxed. I wish I'd stayed with Mary – I need to talk to her for hours and hours, preferably into the next day. Only Adrian would miss her in bed. Men keep women apart, which is why I'm here. I can feel the children's hands on the back of my neck, their cheeks against my lips. I left them happy, playing in the garden with the other girls.

Mary said, 'You don't have to come back on Saturday.' Elisabeth heard her and agreed.

Where did that motor-bike come from, scattering the people crossing the road? It looks as if he was aiming for them, as if he wanted to hit one of them. People are so fragile, so easily damaged. I can see Mary and Adrian with the five children, losing Sally in the panic. And Mary wouldn't be able to contact me. Who knows if there'd be anyone at Bernt's Centre to take a message? I want to go back now. My heart is going too fast. Even Bernt might be knocked down on his way here, if it comes to that. I wouldn't know if he'd stood me up, or if I needed to phone the police. It's already twenty-five to two, and we said half past one. Why the hell am I here? Especially, why the hell did I slip a packet of condoms into my washbag? Because I'm not a naïve twenty-year-old any more. I've got myself and the children to protect. If nothing happens, no-one will know they were there.

Unfinished business, that's why I came. Not sex.

Maybe he's come already, and we didn't recognise each other. The oily, sea-going river throws off the sun. The light is bouncing on the surface of the water. I'm getting too hot, sweating, and my hair is curling tight and sticking to my face, and someone has to walk into me, because I was daring to take up ten per cent of the steps. Bugger him.

'You're still just as blonde.'

I never noticed him coming. His hair and beard are cropped short, and so much grey in them! He's grown up. Well, of course.

We stand there, looking each other up and down. Neither of us knows what to do or say. I remember lunch. He looks relieved.

'I've got this bag – I'll leave it at the *Garderobe*.' There I am already, losing parts of my English and grabbing German words instead.

It seems we're both vegetarians – they're coming out all over the place. There are large posters propped round the entrance hall, showing the collage. Bernt glances at one, smiles at me, then looks concerned. (He sees too much.) Yes, I am scared of going in there, but I said I would, so I will.

The mirrored walls reflect a telescopic sequence of Karins and Bernts, eating salad and French bread, and all talking nervously at once. I find myself watching his face in the second reflection. Our eyes seem to meet there, but that may be an illusion. I must ask him about his work. I feel safer if I can keep him talking.

'You say I can give time, it's precisely time that's the problem. You see, in Germany there is a quota of doctors for any given area, so what do I do, turn people away? It's a constant battle with the system, of course I use alternative therapies – I've trained as an acupuncturist myself. I don't reach for technological diagnostic aids as a matter of course. But to really give the time I'd like to I'd have to exhaust myself, and what good would I be then? As it is –'

His eyes are rather tired, but just as bright, the lashes round them as thick, and the creasing round them is very attractive, especially when he smiles, though according to Donald, my creases – Shut up, Donald. Go fuck yourself.

Bernt says, 'I started as a gynaecologist, till I saw how many of the problems were rooted in the soul. And you had to dismiss that aspect of them, as if the physical symptoms were all that mattered. I was becoming part of the problem.' He moves his hands apologetically. 'You know, Karin, I've always liked caring for people. I would have been happy as a nurse,' (I doubt it) 'but it didn't occur to me when I was studying. What people really need is space, so they can learn how to heal themselves. But – listen, I want to hear about you.'

I'm on. I tell him I'm training to be a herbalist. He says that's wonderful, he likes to use herbal medicines, the whole plant has properties the refined extract doesn't, as well as being gentler, and of course, as a herbalist, I will be able to make space to listen to people, probably without the problems he faces. I'm really meeting his eyes now, telling him what I've learnt. I'd forgotten how his enthusiasm could light me up. Someone squeezes in beside me, holding the catalogue of Anna's exhibition. My throat goes into spasm. Bernt is watching my face. He's puzzling.

Now he asks, 'And your children, did you leave them all right?' It's a diagnostic question.

'Yes, they were quite happy.'

Silence. He sits back. I drink to loosen my throat.

'What are they like, your children?'

I'm losing my breath. Why does this question panic me? I flounder with descriptions. Children are secret creatures anyway. However well you know the seedcase, the adult, sprouting inside, is out of reach. I've got a couple of photographs in my handbag, so I fetch them out. I say, 'It's strange, Sally looks like you.' And at once there rises up a fog of unspoken, tongue-tied emotion.

In a neutral voice he asks, 'And your garden, does it grow good things?'

'It's untidy, but beautiful, and it grows good fruit and vegetables. Yes.'

He says, 'And so you've got what you wanted, your husband, your house, your children, your garden.' He sounds antagonistic, derogatory.

I have to say it, 'I'm divorcing Donald.'

And Bernt says nothing at all.

I shall sell the fabric collage, and invest the money for the children. I wouldn't have it in the house.

I can tell he's irritated with me, because I won't talk. He likes the fabric collage. He loves the photograph of the fence at Greenham. I can't give him my attention: Donald's voice is far louder.

'What the hell is this mess in here? What about dinner, aren't we eating tonight?' (The collage could be the sculpted bark of an old, old tree, brilliantly coloured with lichen, a world for innumerable small creatures.) Meg behind Donald, trying to shut him up, a gaping sack of dressmaking remnants spilling all over the floor, and the cat curled among them, opening one eye at the disturbance, Anna and the collage were all over the kitchen table, and the children were gluing up the chair seats. (Someone is hacking at the trunk.)

Anna: 'I'm taking you out tonight, to that Chinese restaurant.' Meg sneaked off to book the table.

Donald: 'I don't want to go out.'

Anna: 'Then you can stay at home.' And we went, all of us leaving the king to sulk on his own in the house.

Bernt says, 'It's painful for you.'

I nod. He suggests I sit down. He says he'll look on his own. He apologises.

We had such a wonderful time at that restaurant. Sometimes Anna was like that when she'd finished something; euphoric, almost aflame. Yes, aflame. We didn't miss Donald at all. Meg and Anna always got on well. I thought it'd teach Donald. I didn't reckon with just what it taught him.

He'd been drinking, waiting for us to come back, and fourteen years of covert hostility burst into the open. They abused each other and the children cried and Meg went white and silent and horrified, so English as she is. (They've made a bad job of the felling, and the tree is splitting, all the little creatures scattering, crazed, and the flames are coming for them.)

I tried to keep her the next day, when she was so tired, but she wouldn't stay in the house with him. I heard the traffic flash on the radio, and yet I was quite unsuspecting when the policeman came to the door.

Would I have let Donald come with me to identify the body, if he'd offered? He didn't. He left it to Meg. They had her in a drawer, tidily under a sheet, but whatever you do, you can't make dead, burned bodies tidy. (The trunk lies blackened and lifeless on a devastated forest floor). I could see the exposed bones of her face, but the eyes that were responsible for this exhibition were gone. She can't see trees now, or colours, and I can't give her sight.

The people beside me are looking at the collage, but what I can see is the distorted person on a distorted road, her hands holding her head, her mouth open – no. I won't. I don't want electrodes on my head, I must hold down the screams. I'm shaking.

'Shall we go?' He's looking gravely at me. Is that fear in his eyes? It feels better when I stand up and move. I'd like to run. I have to collect my bag. The attendant can't find it. (Spiny wings are beating at my face.) Bernt says we'll take a taxi to the Centre. He'll make me a drink, and we can talk. Do I want to listen to anything more?

This is one of the bedrooms for visiting speakers. It's very comfortable, with a double bed, a bathroom, and a couple of plushy armchairs. He's next door in his own room, putting the kettle on. Deep breathing helps, as they said in the shelters.

Once, when I was small, I was swinging on the banister between the landing and the stairwell, and I went too far. I found myself overbalancing towards the three-storey drop, then my hands were gripped from within, my muscles went hard, and pushed me back.

He asks, 'What would you like to drink?'

'Have you some camomile?'

'Yes.' It was always pleasant to watch him when he mixed drinks and cooked, and that hasn't changed, but this time I feel he's using the task to calm himself. We talk about the Centre. He tells me the founder was in the Vegetarian Society with Gandhi, was interested in theosophy and Eastern religions and yoga, and left his house and all his money in trust to promote self-healing and vegetarianism. There are photographs of India and the Far East on the wall, and Eastern prints. The room is stone-colour and off-white except for the bright pictures and the Liberty curtains. I like it. Only they ruined the plaster ceiling when they built in the bathroom: the flowered and fruited ceiling rose is off-centre. He passes me my tisane, and our hands touch. We drink in silence.

'So, about my grandmother, Bernt.'

He takes a deep breath in. 'I may have got you here on false pretences. Really, apart from my father's story of how she looked after him at the end of the war, I know very little. What my own grandmother told me, she told you, too. But I'm afraid, because she was always a skeleton in the cupboard as far as my mother was concerned –'

I'm raging. I jump up from my seat.

'Damn you, Bernt, how dare you say that? Don't you know she was worth twenty of the sort of smug smart bitches who looked down on her? And of you, too.'

If I were Sally, I'd be able to put my face to the wall.

He looks at the floor. There's something in his face I can't read. 'Karin, I'm sorry, I phrased that badly. I know how much love she gave you. I never agreed with my mother. I know what she gave you, and then to be forcibly sterilised on top of everything else –'

'What did you say? Who told you?'

'Karin, you didn't know?'

'No.' I'd better sit down again. I feel winded.

'My father told me, years ago. I thought you must know.'

I can't bear to look at Bernt: he's a doctor. My mouth is dry.

'When?'

'After her second breakdown.'

It's all too much, tasteless, melodramatic. I feel nauseated, but it's not so easy to throw up the poisons from your soul. If Bernt was only my cousin, if he'd never been my lover, he might put his hand out to me – and I might push it away, because he's a doctor. Not only tasteless and melodramatic, but such a bad joke.

Looking at my knees, I say, 'That's the second shock I've had. A friend of my mother's told me Anna was captured by the Russians and raped for a week. They made her pregnant, and she had an abortion. Did your father tell you that, too? He must have known.'

'No, he never told me that.' He looks shocked and chastened, as if he was accepting responsibility. He says, 'Maybe my father wanted to forget it ever happened. He was so fond of your mother.'

A pause, then, 'I wish my mother had understood.'

'So do I.' The ice is getting thin.

'She sent you her love, by the way.'

Well, I'm safe now, I suppose, married, two children –

'She's got breast cancer. She's going to die.'

I've just been angry with her, now I feel as if I'd struck her tormented body.

'How long has she got?'

'She wouldn't have any treatment: she said she'd rather die with dignity. She wants to join my father. They were married for thirty-eight years, and they were in love for seven years before that. She's never known how to live without him. They said three months.'

'She lived her whole life through him. And you.'

'I know. It's a pity. I'll miss her. But it's her right, you know –'

'I'm sorry, Bernt.'

I can't handle any more, and I don't think he can: this conversation has to stop. It seems he feels so too: he says I look really tired. I admit to a disturbed night with Sally, and the M40, which I hate – I say would he mind if I had a rest before dinner? He says he'll wake me in a couple of hours.

So here is the final twist – Erich came home. Two days before Anna was due to leave for England. Whatever they all expected of each other, none of them found it. Anna was going to marry the enemy. Erich shrugged his shoulders. One more thing he had lost. He had seen what humanity was, or so he believed, had no illusions left when he himself had scuffled and bit and kicked for a handful of raw potato peelings. Only his obstinacy had kept him from worse meanness. I believed Anna when she said he never shopped anyone, out of pure malice, to the Russian guards. But he had learnt not compassion, but contempt. And faith, which was still so important to Helene, was a currency forever devalued. There were plenty of others like him. He wanted comfort, prosperity, food and drink, and was prepared to work like blazes to hang onto it. Monika helped him get a new job in Cologne.

And for a while, it must have been invaluable to have a wife who had learned to be tough, who knew how to survive and make something out of what I would regard as refuse. But things got better, and by the time I was born he was able to buy them a country house. Her crinkly ball of wool, her old clothes, her work-knobbled hands must have begun to annoy him. She wasn't interested in elegance any more. She looked like a peasant woman, and she laboured in the garden and the orchard, dirt on her hands. Erich began to spend some weekends, as well as weekdays, in Cologne. He said he had work to do. Monika warned Helene, and Helene shook her head and wouldn't listen. When Anna brought us to visit, he was there. Of course he wanted her to think everything was all right. And Helene said nothing.

I imagine Helene was content to be alone, with the soil and the wind in the trees, feeling her own strength and the capability of her hands. I think she liked to have Erich away. But did the dead embryo haunt her, did she brood on her sin? I can imagine her in church, afraid to confess or communicate.

When he did come home, I suppose he took her, and complained about her appearance. Was she testing him, to see if he was interested in herself rather than her body? And was it also an act of revenge? She had wanted babies and disliked sex, and she'd been forced to have sex without babies. To emphasise Erich's point, the authorities had spayed her as you might a bitch or a cat.

It must have taken courage, to refuse him sex. But she'd given him his opening. Quick, easy, the vindication of male rights. The law was on his side.

She left the lawyer's letter for him to open, as she did all other official mail. The same with the notice of the divorce, which she hadn't defended. When the dust grew too thick on the letters, she went looking for him, and the woman who came to the door laughed at her and said she was now his wife.

Helene began to weep and scream, but Erich knew how to silence that inconvenient voice.

I found the letter from the mental hospital among Anna's papers. It accuses her of sleeplessness, lack of interest in self and others, depression, excessive fits of crying, religious mania. She saw visions. They couldn't have that. She might have stayed there for ever, but she managed to smuggle a letter out to Anna, and Anna rescued her.

I wish I could cry.

22

This food is good. I haven't had Indian vegetarian before. I may regret the wine. For the moment, I'm enjoying it, it's making everything seem slightly unreal, and the bits of stuffed and puffed pastry are delicious. There's something about such a meal that slows you down of itself.

The fairy-lights round the hanging gilt lamps are innocent, child-Christmassy. This must have been a vault once. I wonder what they kept here?

'Bernt?'

'Yes?'

'Do you think I'm crazy? Trying to relive her life. Not even writing it down. Donald would have understood better if I'd written it.'

'He thought you were crazy?'

'He wanted me to have analysis.'

'Do you want to write it down?'

'No, I don't need to.' And do I need to put Bernt through these sort of hoops?

The waiters' faces are like roast coffee against their white collars, very pleasing. They move in and out, deftly, discreetly. Do they notice us, I wonder? The little bulb in the lamp casts a kindly light on Bernt's long nose and bright dark eyes. His lips are rather full, in among the grizzled curls of moustache and beard, wet with wine. The hand he's not eating with lies quiet on the table.

'No-one would guess you were German, Bernt.' Definitely the wine has affected me: I no longer quite care what I say.

'Well, my grandfather was a Frenchman.'

'You don't look like him.'

'How do you know?' He makes the sort of face he used to make at me in our childhood. 'Did you ever get my grandmother to describe him?'

I laugh. 'No.'

'As for you, Karin, tall, blonde, blue-eyed, you look like every German's idea of an Englishwoman, and every English person's idea of a German.'

'In other words, I don't fit in anywhere.' I wish I could shut up. 'You know, Bernt, you were the lucky one. Being in Germany, that Nazi past was something you could rebel against.'

'I was lucky I knew anything about it, being in Germany. Plenty of our contemporaries didn't.'

'No, but listen,' (do I want him to?) 'what I had was the idealisation of a war I felt had been fought against me. I identified with the whole of Germany, Nazi past and all. But I was supposed to be British.'

The waiter brings the main course. Bernt sits looking at me, saying nothing and considering.

'It's not so easy for any of us to shrug off, Karin. What about my grandfather? He believed in the Third Reich till the day he died. Of course, you don't know. I began to visit him in his old people's home when I was doing my alternative service.'

'Where did you do it?'

'It was a geriatric hospital – a bad one. That's how I began to think about him. He wasn't far away. So I went to see him, and he was delighted. He'd quite forgotten he didn't like me, I was his male descendant.' Bernt makes the monkey-grimace again. 'Mind you, he told me what a shame it was I had this colouring, and that hair on my arms and hands, he said it didn't look Aryan.'

The wine is a little gold lens at the bottom of the bottle. Bernt asks if I want to share another. I think I'll be safer with mango juice. I wish he hadn't drawn my attention to his arms and hands: the wine has already weakened my superego, and the subconscious is poking memories at me.

'Why did you really go?' (Keep him talking.)

'Part of it was that, like you, I wanted to find out. It wasn't difficult to get him to talk about it all.'

'What did he do, Bernt?'

'Oh, what he did was really quite uninteresting – he was a little bureaucrat – he filled in forms and people died. He was actually ashamed of not having played a more active part, even though that saved his life after the war. He thought it was disgraceful that he was sent to prison. It was his attitude that interested me.'

'I thought he only joined up because he was afraid, because he'd been beaten up once for looking Jewish.'

'The true story was a little more complicated than that. Oh yes, he was jumped on one night: when he screamed that he wasn't a Jew, they laughed – that's what they all say, little Aaron. So he had a brilliant idea: he offered to take his trousers down so they could see for themselves. They took him up on it. Mind you, what they promised him they'd do if they found he'd been circumcised, you can imagine for yourself. It hurts my masculinity too much to think about it, even though I am a doctor. In any case, they found out he was speaking the truth: it was all there. What impressed him was how apologetic they were, they bought him a drink, and he bought them one, and in the end they all rolled home together – pissed as newts, I think you say? So he thought they were great fellows, and he decided to join the SS, an adjunct, no more. He wasn't big enough or tough enough for a bully-boy, and in fact it was his ordinary work as a civil servant that he was jailed for.'

The drinks arrive, my mango juice and Perrier for him.

He says, 'Well, you know, it's not easy to go against the whole of society.'

'You did.'

'As did your mother. But in a relatively benign situation – the Army is a dictatorship, of course, and they threatened me and abused me and kicked me once or twice, though some of them were tolerant – no-one was going to kill me or torture me. Actually the worst thing was the feeling of being a nuisance, of having to explain myself to people who weren't convinced by me. I don't know if I would have been brave, in those days.'

'How long did you go on visiting your grandfather?'

'About three months. Then he asked me if I'd done my military service yet. I tried to avoid the question, but he was quite insistent. So I had to tell him I wasn't doing it, that I was looking after old people instead. He was furious. He ordered me out of the room. He said it was disgusting, his grandson refusing to fight for his country and waiting on old people who'd have been put out of their misery a long time ago in a properly organised world. I needn't emphasise the irony. That night he had a heart attack and died. So there you are. Peter helped bring on your grandmother's death by coming home in a uniform, I did the same by my grandfather when I refused to put on a uniform.' He smiles bitterly and stares at the encrusted rough-painted wall behind me.

'How did you feel about it?'

'The strange thing was, Karin, I actually got quite fond of the old devil. I used to bring him cigarettes, and make him comfortable – they weren't bad, in that home, but there was always something extra I could do. I just used to pretend to need the toilet quickly if he started to sing his old songs. I was very unhappy that he died like that. I cried.'

I'm shaken by his openness. His hand is still on the table, and I put mine out to his – maybe I have had too much wine, but it feels right. He puts his other hand to mine, and while I stroke his wrist and the back of his hand, rediscovering the texture of his skin, his fingers move up and down the underside of my wrist, go under the rolled edge of my shirt sleeve, and come back to stroke the palms of my hands.

Don't let's talk any more, let's just touch each other, without asking what it might mean.

Now there is nothing but the two of us, at the door of my room – I can't remember how we got here. Inside, it's quiet and blank, like a page waiting for the words. I feel the weight of his body against mine, taste him, smell him. They used to say urgency was male, but I'm racing like a child pursued, trying to reach home. Here's the scar he got falling down the stairs at Monika's. It runs under his beard –

'You did grow the beard to hide the scar, admit it now, Bernt.'

'*Quatsch*, I didn't. Why waste time shaving?'

'I don't believe you. Bernt –'

'Yes?'

'I've got something – in my bag –'

'Well, good. Now I don't have to get what I bought, just in case.'

I have to laugh. 'So neither of us is ingenuous any more.'

'Well, you know, Karin, one gets older, one has to behave like a responsible person at last – though it might reassure you to know I've never succeeded in being really promiscuous, and over the last years –'

His naked skin is warm against mine, the bedcover cool under my back.

'And Ulrike? And Donald?'

'Very true.'

But why did I have to introduce Donald's name, it was Donald I was running from, and he's managed to ambush me from the side. Will I be able to –

'What's wrong?'

No, it's got to be all right this time, just don't let me lose the momentum.

'I don't want to talk about it now.'

He's pulling away from me. 'Shit. Shit, shit, shit.'

I feel frustrated, furious, panicky; I want to bite.

Angrily, he says, 'Karin, I don't know what games you played with your husband, but I'm not starting where he left off. You won't make me into your rapist.'

'You know all about me, do you?' I still want to dig my teeth in, my nails too, yet I feel sick again.

'I don't know anything about you. How can I? You've been playing hide-and-seek with me, drawing me out, keeping me out.'

I feel trapped. I hate it that I'm naked.

'You're afraid of me. You've been through hell this afternoon, but you don't trust me enough to share it. You're lying here with me, you'll do what you're afraid of, then you can tell yourself men are all the same.'

'And you, of course, you've no ulterior motive. You're not angry with me for what I did to you when I married Donald. You're above all that with your open relationships and the space you give women. Maybe you've just found a subtler way of manipulating them.'

I recognise the nausea now, it's the choking feeling you get from a tube down your throat, when they anaesthetise you and paralyse you and breathe for you – your body remembers how it was invaded, and the sensation stays with you when you wake up. I hate it.

He says, 'You think I'm so sure of my ground? I've often asked myself that last question.'

'Yes, you're ideologically correct, aren't you? You always had to be. It's just as well for you. Take a better look and see what you escaped, what a mess your clever colleagues left me in. Sterility is far more becoming, isn't it?' I'm turning my teeth on myself now, it's an ugly satisfaction. I know what to do: put my ankles together and my knees apart for the doctor to see, go floppy. 'Go on, Herr Doktor. I want you to see. I expect you've examined hundreds of women's fannies by now, haven't you?'

'Karin,' he says, 'Karin.' His voice is shaking, he's beginning to cry as naturally as a woman. He won't get comfort from me: I'm shivering with fury. And yet I'm appalled at what I've done, no woman ought to do this to a man – no, I won't think that. He's crying, and I can't. It's not fair. He can permit his emotions, he's not afraid of a ravenous whirlpool inside him.

In my mind, a voice that resembles my own says coldly: she's cracking up.

Has it been worth it, all this trawling in the past? It hasn't helped me. I should never have uncovered those deep fissures, those irreparable structural defects. My bag is still sitting at the side of the bed: I'll get my dressing gown.

He says, 'When I read your letter, I thought you needed something I could give you. Was I wrong?'

Abruptly, I snap, 'The last few times I had intercourse with Donald, it was excruciating.'

'Do you know why?' He sounds like a doctor, but he's wiping his eyes and nose with his hand like a baby. Oh, he has ways past my defences, hasn't he?

'I was tense, and dry.'

'Perhaps it would have been helpful if I'd known about it.'

'I don't want you to be my therapist.'

'So I have to be a doctor. Nothing else. Is it just because I'm a man that you think I couldn't care for you without being a professional?'

I don't answer, because I don't know if it's true.

He says, 'You'd better turn to women, like Ulrike.'

'Has she?' Even with the dressing gown, I'm cold.

'Yes. It's a political decision. She says it's nothing against me.'

Poor Bernt. He's spent years working on himself, only to be told he'll never make it after all.

I've come to a full stop. I can only babble rubbish and clichés. Or I could say I don't blame Ulrike, which would be true, but not for the obvious reason. I lay myself down on the bed, closing my eyes and glad of the dark. After all that energy lost, we're nowhere.

His hand touches the back of my neck, stroking it gently. A huge breath escapes from me, shakes me as it leaves.

'Do you want me to carry on?'

'Yes.' He didn't hear me. 'Yes.'

His fingers massage the strained-tight muscles in my neck, move further down my back, under my dressing gown. My body is easing itself, I'm losing my defences – they were already undermined, yet I find I'm clutching them as they slip away from me. His hands are holding me.

He says, 'Let it come, Karin.' But I couldn't weep if I didn't hear him crying too: my pain and his pain connect us as nothing else has today.

'Bernt, when I was a little girl, Peter used to run away from me, with his coat spread out like wings, and I'd be left behind. And if I was out with my father, I never knew if he'd pick me up and carry me, or if I'd be left to struggle after him – Bernt, you're still angry with me, aren't you?'

'I've no right to be angry. Karin, what I didn't tell when we talked about Tante Helene was why my father told me what happened to her. I was depressed, after you left. In the end I had psychotherapy. He thought at first I'd snap out of it, if he was angry. He couldn't cope with me at all. He shouted at me that I could afford to indulge myself, not like her – Yes, you're right. I was angry. When you said Sally looks like me –'

He asks, 'Please, Karin, don't let us talk for a while.'

We reach our hands out to feel for each other, as if we were blind.

'Bernt, do you think they sterilised her without an anaesthetic?'

He shudders. 'I don't know, Karin. I hope not. They weren't all Mengeles, you know. I'm sorry, Karin. I understand how you feel about doctors. At least I think so.' He says, 'I really had no right to be angry. You were free.'

'Freedom is something people are very ready to define on behalf of everyone else – I need to find out for myself what it means to me. I wasn't free then. I know that, I'm glad you were angry. It makes you real.'

He says, 'My father was a rescuer. I suppose I've inherited it from him. But he locked my mother in. Or maybe she was already in chains. I couldn't rescue her, and I haven't succeeded with anyone else. I've had to learn to keep the white horse in the field – that isn't easy.'

'I'm sure the horse likes it better in the field.'

He laughs shakily. 'I'm tired.'

The dark claims us both, fetching us to sleep, like children, on its breast.

'So, you're awake. Are you hungry?'

He's sitting in one of the armchairs with a newspaper. He's dressed, wearing jeans and a T-shirt. He puts the paper down on the floor and smiles at me.

'I went out to get us something to eat. There's a little shop on the corner.'

'What have you got?'

'Croissants and rolls and peach jam – no, stay there. Are you warm enough?'

'I don't want to be naked when you're not. It has certain sado-masochistic overtones –'

'When you put it like that, what can I say? Have your dressing gown. Here, let me –' He arranges my pillows. I feel languid and pleasurably heavy, as I used to when Omi did my hair. He puts the kettle on and prepares the food. As I watch him, it's as if his hands were caressing me.

Sleepily, I say, 'I'm being spoilt.'

'Isn't it nice to be spoilt?'

'Very nice, but I haven't earned it.'

He frowns. 'How would you earn it?'

'By being ill, or having a baby, or a birthday. Oh, and there's Mothering Sunday.'

'Well, today you're having breakfast in bed because it pleases me. Will you let it please *you* now?'

'It's not difficult, Bernt.'

He relaxes, and puts the kettle on to make a drink.

'Where did you filch the crockery?'

'There's a kitchenette next door. I've been using it all week.'

'So we'll have to wash up.'

'Not you.'

'Bernt, would you like me to stay till tomorrow?'

He claims he wants to visit the Tower of London and Madame Tussaud's. I say he can go without me. He says he now sees it was a mistake to spoil me, and have I any alternative suggestions? I ask him if he's forgotten I was brought up in London? I plan the day. We walk through the streets and parks to Kensington, and I show him a gallery of netsuke, tiny kimono ornaments, little ivory frogs and smiling dark wood immortals, yawning or barking red dogs. It's a place Anna and I visited last year. We were happy together. Now Bernt and I laugh, pointing out the details that are so easy to miss – this is an oblique way of making love. He knows that, too.

I show him the lovely Chelsea hospital and we walk down to the river afterwards. We stand on the bank. Behind us the traffic grinds and snarls. It's low tide, and the river is slouching between mud banks. Its ugly boats pull against the current and strain their anchor ropes.

I say, 'I like to feel the city like this, mile after mile of it. Then I like to get out of it. When I come back to Oxford, it's a pleasure to find it asleep.'

'I've never been to Oxford.' I can't respond, not yet. He says, 'Germany hasn't got a capital, not like London. How could it? Bonn is a provincial city among other provincial cities. Berlin is an anomaly and a conference and recreation centre.'

'Have you been there again?'

'Oh yes. And in the East. I love Berlin.'

Our hands join, and we walk along in silence. Again, I feel we are two children, maybe a sister and brother who've somehow got lost.

'Bernt, do you believe in God?'

'I don't know.'

We keep walking. Seagulls draw wide, airborne arcs, dipping to the river, turning, winging, never a straight line, their cries, by contrast, ragged, snatched out of the traffic roar.

'Bernt, if we go on, we'll hurt each other again.'

'Yes. Do you want to?'

'Yes, I think so. Yes. And you?'

He frowns. 'I can't have done with you, it seems, you've always fascinated me from the time we were two small children caught naked in the bathroom together. You were such a pretty little girl, with your blonde curls and your blue eyes, but that wasn't it.'

'And when we met next – was it two years later? I wouldn't speak to you. Were you as embarrassed as I was?'

We're laughing, running, still holding hands.

'Karin, you really want me to come in?'

'I do want you. I wouldn't otherwise. Please believe me, Bernt.'

He lies beneath me, watching my face. I kiss his eyes shut. 'It's all right, Bernt. It's all right.'

He's within me, under me, his hands on me, something overcoming me that feels like grief as much as pleasure, Bernt, my brother, my lover. I'm lost now, it's beautiful, why am I crying?

'Bernt, I believe there is a God, only it's inside every one of us.'

'Karin, I love you. I love you, Karin.'

The old words, easily said. Maybe not.

23

The children are asleep in the back of the car, clutching the chocolate Bernt bought for them. Bribery and corruption, probably appropriate. Nothing will be easy.

It feels as if I'd spent seven years in fairyland, to re-emerge at the moment I vanished. It feels as if I'd never been away. The two worlds are moving together uneasily in my mind. My life is becoming such a complex web – then the tensions will only be a problem if they're unequal. This image seems marvellously helpful – till the light fades from it, and I wonder why I was so pleased?

I'll have to put this car up for sale. Luckily it's in my name.

I'm still wearing the wedding ring Donald gave me. If I slow down, I ought to be able to take it off safely. Helene wore her wedding ring till it cracked in half. After Erich's death, Sybille released the ring Helene gave him, but why did he keep it? She was buried with that ring. There, it's off. Is it mine, or Donald's? It's quite valuable, I ought to sell it.

No.

I hope the children wake when the car stops. I'm tired. I don't want to half-carry Sally. There are a lot of cars parked in our road. There are people in them. This is scary, as if several spies are watching the house. They are watching me, they're getting out of their cars as they see me turn into the drive, as I put the handbrake on there are about five of them crowding round my door.

'Mummy, who are all these people?' Elisabeth, waking, sounds frightened.

'I don't know. Sally, darling, wake up.'

'She's sat on the chocolate Uncle Bernt sent her. It's all over her dress, and the seat.'

Sally wakes up and wails about her chocolate. I will occupy myself with the children, I won't be intimidated. (I wish I didn't have to open the door.)

They're there, like a flight of vultures, they're journalists, all asking questions at once, they represent the 'Daily Shit' and the 'Tabloid Crap'. 'Mrs Lowe, what do you think about your husband's involvement in biological warfare projects?' 'Mrs Lowe, do you think your husband will be going to jail?' 'Mrs Lowe, where is your husband at present?' I might have guessed. And the children have to hear all this for the first time from this purulent bunch.

Snarling at them, I battle my way to the door, pulling Sally who is half-asleep and crying about her chocolate, my arm painfully burdened by my overnight bag, Elisabeth with her own and Sally's things, and of course, now that I've slammed the door on the fingers of the most persistent, the violin is still in the car, and I'll have to go out and fetch it.

The journalists bray and push against me. I dive into the car for the fiddle, hating to feel my bum exposed, come out and almost crack my head against two of them, make a dart for the house – and one of them manages to get in the door with me. He's pink and plump with upturned nostrils. He looks like the plaster pigs that used to stand in butchers' windows, skipping obscenely with a rope of sausages.

'Get out.' Dare I spit at him?

He's too intent on his own business to react. Probably he's already flattened me onto a piece of paper and reduced me to his own dimensions. (I stand by my husband, says blonde mother-of-two Karin Lowe.)

'Mrs Lowe –'

'I'm not Mrs Lowe.'

That's stumped him.

Sally opens her mouth and says, 'My Mummy doesn't use Daddy's name. She's Dr Birkett.'

Thank you Sally. The ears flap, there is a grunt, and he plunges straight at his feed: he's here to find out if I know about Donald's work on a biological warfare project in Brazil which has, it appears, gone wrong, and fifty people have died of some vile virus. (The important work Donald was doing for the US government.)

I've had enough. 'If you don't get out, I'll call the police.'

You'd think this was the most amazing thing anyone could possibly tell him. His cheeks are flushing in outraged astonishment. He asks how the children would react if Donald were successfully prosecuted by the Brazilian government, who are talking about prison sentences for all concerned? Sally bursts into tears. I want to kill him. He stinks, pigs do, especially male chauvinist ones. I've seen his newspaper round potatoes and cabbages (Busty Sharron's a real teaser, especially with her naughty knickers on).

He's launching into something else. I'm going to ignore him. Nine, nine, nine. The emergency operator answers and asks which service I want. I tell her. The reporter asks when Donald is due home. Please, Sally, don't tell him. Thank you, Elisabeth, but I can't bear to hear Sally howling and squabbling as you drag her away. The police come on the line and I explain to them that a reporter has forced his way into my house and won't leave – will they please come and remove him? The reporter asks how many times Donald has been away in the past year. The police promise action, so I put the receiver down and tell the reporter they're coming. He asks me if I have a good relationship with Donald? Why don't I keep a large savage dog? The cat is actually rubbing herself against the hog's legs, promiscuous creature that she is. If Donald were here, I could kill him at the same time. That'd give the police and reporters something to get busy with. I sharpened the kitchen knife on Thursday. The reporter carries on with increasingly insolent questions, then dodges out of the door when he hears the police coming up the drive – the local bobby, he comes to the children's school and gives them pep-talks about not speaking to strangers. I have to explain to him what all this is about, and he looks slightly askance at me. I'm included in Donald's shame. Bloody hell, I've had enough shame.

Sally won't stop crying. She doesn't want her father to go to prison. She says it's my fault, for sending him away. Elisabeth stands there, tall, dark, serious and uncommunicative.

'Are you worried, Elisabeth?'

'I'm not going to make things worse for you.'

'Please, Elisabeth, don't. If you want to scream, scream, Elisabeth. Why don't you smash a full milk bottle? I wouldn't mind the mess.'

'No.'

At least the bobby cleared the reporters out of the garden and into their cars, and, I don't believe it, an engine is being switched on, yes, and the whole flotilla is departing in convoy. Even the pig.

They would have been richly rewarded for patience, it can only be half an hour since they went, and here is Donald, stopping his black Audi in the drive (as much of a cliché as my Volvo; I can't wait to get rid of it). I'd better not murder him, though, it would ruin the children's lives and I'd hate to spend the rest of mine in prison. He's early. He's not due back from the States yet. From the look of him, he came back today. I expect there was a posse at the airport to meet him. He brushes past the pink geraniums in the tub by the front door, knocking one of the flowers off. His good-looking sulky face is handsomer and sulkier than ever (he really is far more beautiful than Bernt) and his shirt is hanging open at the neck in an uncared-for way. There's a double crease in one of his trouser legs, the poor man, without a woman to look after him, didn't Martha oblige? She's got sense, mistresses oughtn't to do ironing.

He's reaching for the bell as I open the door.

'Oh, there you are.'

He slams the door behind him. The children come downstairs to see who it is. Sally winds her arms round his legs, begging him not to go to prison (she seems to think he has a choice), and Elisabeth, having kissed him, draws off abruptly, looking stricken.

'You've heard, then.'

'I had to get the police to clear out the reporters.'

'They've been here too? My God.'

'When did you get back?'

'Today. Karin, I don't want to get divorced.'

'What?'

'You heard me. I want to come back here to live.'

I could say he has no right to make the decision without me. I could easily say I don't want him. But he looks so natural in this house, and he's the children's father. The very fact that I don't want him half-convinces me he must be right. How dare I ask for what I want, cries Guilt, standing right behind me and strident in my ear.

'Donald –'

'Yes?'

I won't be able to speak, my mouth is drying up.

'No, Donald.' That hurt. And he looks so pathetic, tired and jetlagged. 'Why do you want to come back?'

'Can't you see that? I need you. I need your support, and if they can say you've ditched me because of this business – it's going to be pretty bad for me. I think it'll be all right in the end. The chances are they'll never get their act together to prosecute us.'

'How many of you are involved?'

'The whole firm, virtually, though as a director I'm particularly responsible. But it'll take years, and the US will probably bring pressure to bear on them to drop it.'

'That man who rang up – he was an investigative reporter, I suppose.'

'Yes. He's the one who ferreted the story out and published it this morning. My coming back early has nothing to do with it. It was just bad luck for me the British newspapers found out what flight I was on. If it hadn't got out, maybe nothing would have happened from the South American end – I don't know.'

'How many people died?'

'About fifty. I'm not sure.'

'How did they come to die?'

He's in the dock. The glass in the door is the stained glass of an old courtroom, myself the prosecutor, the children the jury. He's afraid.

'It was purely for defence purposes, Karin.' He looks like a trapped animal. I remember how they botched the hangings after Nuremberg. 'We've been working on a new agent we think the Russians have got; it's important to develop protective clothing that can give an adequate shield against it. Well, there was a lot of hassle about the place in the States where the work was scheduled: someone got hold of it and spread a panic among the local people, so we had to move to this site in Brazil. Unfortunately, the engineers there didn't build the equipment to specification, and somehow it wasn't checked up properly, I don't know how I missed it. The agent leaked into a stream, and contaminated the drinking water. There's no cure. Fortunately it was only a small community, and the virus hasn't got a long lifespan.'

'So they all died?'

'Don't look at me like that. Yes.'

'And you were actually responsible, you had some role in checking the equipment.' I have no right to prosecute, I'm guilty, too –

'I had to approve it, yes. It was very unfortunate. You don't seem to realise how much strain I've been under, Karin, it was in a good cause. We have to defend ourselves. If the Russians have these things –'

They all died.

He asks the children, 'Wouldn't you like me to come back with you again?'

'Yes,' says Sally.

'No,' says Elisabeth, white-faced.

Relentlessly, I say, 'Unfortunate, you call it. Not criminal. Just unfortunate.'

'Karin, you're talking about a country where life is cheap. You have no idea –'

'Donald, get out.'

Forgotten is justice, forgotten the courtroom. I can't bear him.

Sally is weeping and screaming and hanging onto Donald's legs again, Donald looks as if he'd like to murder me. I'm frightened of his hands. Well, I thought he was a killer. I was right, wasn't I, if it was only by default? But aren't we all? (If Erich had gone to America, he'd probably have ended up working on the Hiroshima bomb.) Guilt slips me a glossy image of a good, forgiving woman who'd take Donald back (repudiating her incestuous liaison with her cousin) and, through her sacrifice, sort him out. I can't. I won't. I ask him why he can't get support from Martha, and he says he doesn't know who I'm talking about. Am I going mad? I can hardly breathe in here, but I can't get to the door to fling it open.

The phone rings. Bernt. He's ringing from Heathrow to say goodbye. I say I can't talk now, please will he ring later, I don't mind how late. Donald is watching and listening. Has he guessed? Will he be the one to run amok with a kitchen knife? I could ring the police again, but they won't interfere in a domestic quarrel, and Interpol, according to him, will take a long time to turn up.

It's I who am stepping forward, taking Donald by the shoulders and walking him towards the door. Sally is sitting in a heap, weeping heartbrokenly. It's my hands that are violent, homicidally strong. Donald is letting me push him out, his face grey, shocked, passive, defeated. He doesn't even try to resist. What's happening seems unreal, slow-motion. He says nothing. I say nothing.

He walks down the drive to his car, gets his keys out, opens the door and starts the engine, routinely putting his seat belt on, drives away in the black car. It feels as if I've killed him, as if he were lying in the back of the car, going away for ever. Guilt shrieks: supposing he disappears, supposing he kills himself?

Elisabeth insists on the television news, and there is the item. There, worse still, is the village of empty, decaying houses, there are the rough, panicky mass graves. Here is Donald, making evasive statements at the airport. They've been too obviously rehearsed, and he comes across as shifty, untrustworthy. The violin sounds sharp and discordant in Sally's room, squeaking off the strings, sawing at my nerves. I've no control over what's happening, I ought to have stopped Elisabeth watching this. The television switches to some more recent deaths: a car bomb in Lebanon.

'Poor Mummy,' says Elisabeth, switching the news off. She's still too pale. 'Mummy, I've got a headache.'

'Do you want something for it?'

'No.'

The violin is crying upstairs, suddenly Sally is playing with more feeling and beauty than any beginner has a right to express.

Sharply, Elisabeth says, 'Mummy, play your guitar.'

'Then you won't hear Sally.'

'I want you to play your guitar. And then we can sing.' She gets up and shuts the door. I'm dismayed, but I won't stop her.

Fifty bodies decaying in the earth. The same toll as one car bomb, and does life come more expensive over here?

'What do you want to sing?'

'Anything.'

I can think of nothing but 'You'll never get to heaven on a sabre jet'. Elisabeth attempts it, and starts to sob.

'Come here, love.'

'No, I'm going to sing.'

I can talk to Bernt when he rings me. If he's read an evening paper I might not even have to explain the filthy business to him. And if he was killed on the autobahn, in the plane? The world is crawling with death. Elisabeth wants me to try a pop song, all about peace and love. It does me good to work out the accompaniment, though the trite words manage to make me cry.

I love Bernt, he's a part of my life I've denied too long, but his loss wouldn't destroy me. That's a cold, comfortless rock

185

of a fact. Well, what am I asking for? Certainty? Reassurance?

'Elisabeth, let me play alone for a while.'

She listens.

'What is it?'

'I'm making it up.'

Here it is, my own theme among so many complex creative generations of women. Of whom I am a part, as they are in me.

Look, there is a pattern, but it modifies as it goes through.